# Andy & Mark and the Time Machine: The Battle of Trenton

Andy & Mark and the Time Machine Series

# Andy & Mark and the Time Machine: The Battle of Trenton

W. F. Reed

Writers Club Press
San Jose New York Lincoln Shanghai

**Andy & Mark and the Time Machine: The Battle of Trenton**



Writers Club Press
an imprint of iUniverse, Inc.

For information address:
iUniverse, Inc.
5220 S. 16th St., Suite 200
Lincoln, NE 68512
www.iuniverse.com

ISBN: 0-595-23587-5

Printed in the United States of America

# Dedication

*This book is dedicated to my parents, Dorothy and Ignatius Reed, who impressed upon me the value of a good education, the discipline to keep moving forward, and the freedom to follow my passions.*

# Contents

# Preface

The Declaration of Independence, approved by Congress on July 4, 1776, pronounced that the United States of America was a free and independent nation; however, what was claimed by the pen had yet to be won by the sword. In the five months that followed, the Continental army had not fared well in its attempt to drive the British from the colonies. In August of that year, General George Washington's army was badly beaten on Long Island, New York. In September, it was driven from New York City. By November, it was on the run in New Jersey, and early December found it fleeing across the Delaware River to escape into Pennsylvania. Battlefield losses, enlistment expirations, and desertions reduced the Continentals to a shadow of the strength that Washington commanded during those heady days in early July. Morale was low and still more enlistments were set to expire at the end of the year.

The predicament of the colonies prompted a recent immigrant from England to write a pamphlet entitled *The Crisis*. In it, Thomas Paine reminded the new republic that great causes require great suffering, and that freedom obtained cheaply was of little value. Like *Common Sense* before it, *The Crisis* served to ignite the fighting spirit throughout the country. General Washington had it read to what was left of his battered forces. It had a positive affect, and army morale improved, but Washington knew that he needed more than fine words and inspiration to hold the Revolution together. He needed a victory. And he needed it before 1776 was over.

*"It may be doubted whether so small a number of men ever employed so short a space of time with greater and more lasting results upon the history of the world."*

*Sir George Otto Trevelyan, British Historian–1903*

# Acknowledgements

A special thanks to Ann Chick for all her help in critiquing and editing the manuscript.

Cover designed by Veronica Johansson.

# The Battle of Trenton – Dec. 26, 1776

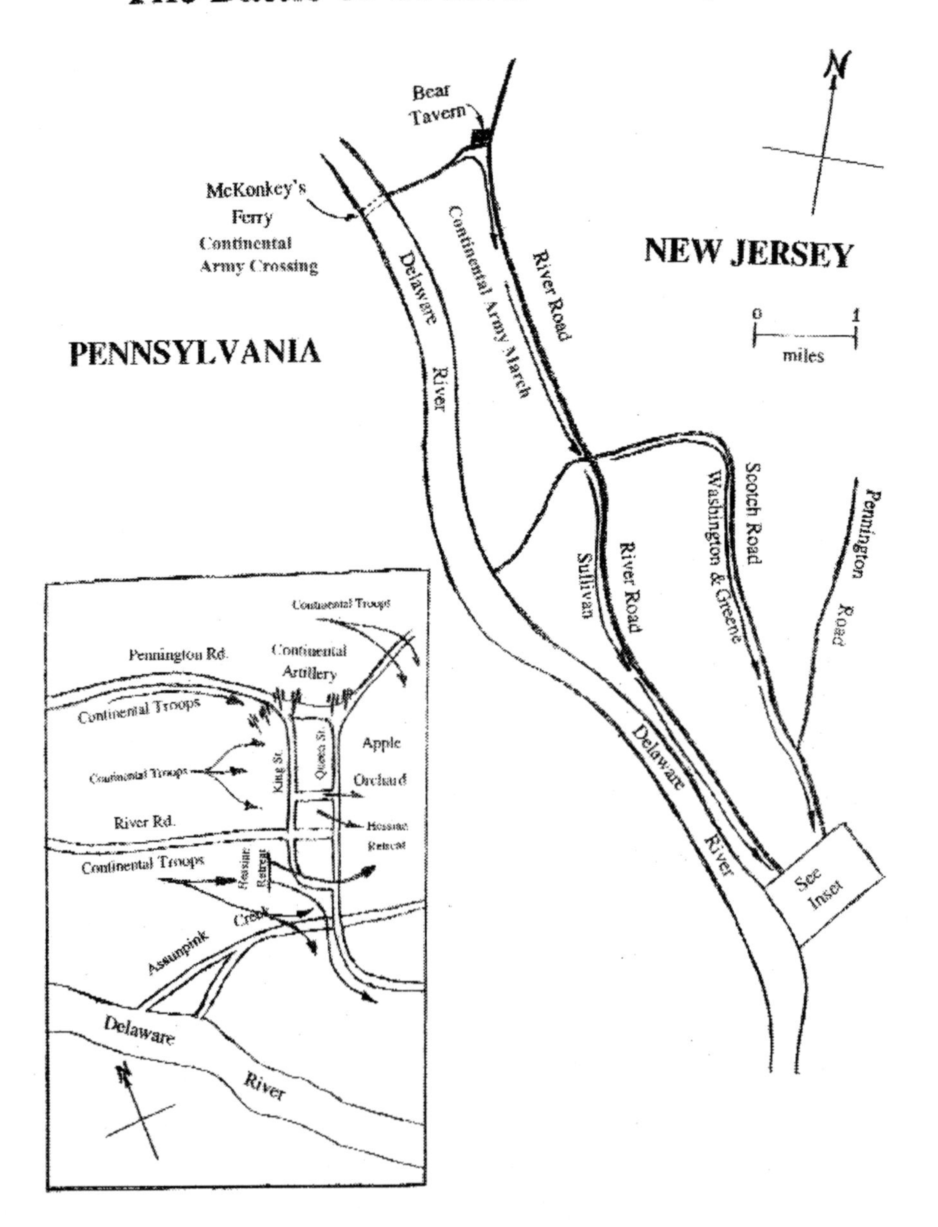

# Chapter 1—Trial And Error

"One last adjustment and that ought to do it," Andy's dad said, as he typed the finishing touches on his revised program for the transporter. We still call it the transporter even though recently we discovered that it did a lot more. My best friend, Andy Royce, and I had tested an earlier version of the program a month before and had discovered a slight flaw. Well, not a flaw exactly but more of an oversight. The device that Andy's dad built in his basement was designed to transport an object from a specially built platform to the coordinates of any geographical point that a user cared to enter. If you wanted to send a book to a friend in California, all you had to do was place the book on the platform, enter the longitude and latitude of your friend's house, and start the program.

There was one minor problem. The book would go to the coordinates of your friend's house all right, but it might not arrive there at the *time* that you wanted. That's what Andy and I discovered when we used it, except that instead of testing it with a book or some other object, we tested it with *me*! It was an accident of course. I never intended to play the guinea pig in such an untested technology. Andy and I had reserved that honor for the Royces' family cat, and we prepared an experiment that went something like this:

First, Andy programmed Gettysburg, Pennsylvania as the target destination because, as history buffs, we knew that a Civil War re-enactment was taking place on the battlefield that day. Second, I prepared a message and attached it to the cat's collar asking the reader to announce his position out loud. We picked one of Mr. Royce's voice transmitters, which we also tied to the collar, so that we could hear the reader's response. The idea was that someone would find the cat and announce his position–thereby confirming that the little fuzzball had indeed arrived at Gettysburg.

The last step was to initiate the program and send the cat on his way. After that, all we had to do was sit and wait for the transmission. Easy. At least it should have been. Unfortunately, Andy mistakenly started the transport sequence shortly after I stepped onto the platform with the cat. When the green fog settled, the cat and I were in Gettysburg!

We'd made the trip unharmed, but I quickly discovered that we'd moved through time as well as space, and we arrived in Gettysburg on the evening of July 2, 1863–just before the final day of the most famous battle in American history!

Our plan was half-baked and poorly executed, and we'd acted on it without any input from Mr. Royce, but the adventure was incredible! I met with the general in command of the Union Army of the Potomac and told him that the Confederates were preparing a major offensive for the next day. Then I got stuck at the front line and saw Confederate General Pickett's charge as it took place! A nineteenth-century assault, complete with the roar of cannon and the crack of musketry! I also saw the ghastly sights of death and heard the screams of the wounded rend the air as the smoke cleared. It's fair to say that I'll never forget the experience, but fortunately, the episode was short-lived. By some quirk of physics, that is still unclear to us, the disruption in space and time was only temporary, and I was returned to my original starting point–the platform in Andy's cellar–twenty-four hours later. And although the cat and I were split up early, we returned at roughly the same time.

In essence, we could call the device a time machine, except that we don't have any control over the *time* part. Andy and his dad's theory is that once an object, or in my case a person, is dematerialized at the platform, he moves into a space / time river whose eddies and currents flow according to the programmed destination. The theory doesn't explain why I ended up at exactly July 2, 1863, but we accept the fact that as a river the flow is *downstream* or *back* in time. We still haven't proven that for sure, though.

Oh, one more thing. I kept the transmitter with me during my stay in Gettysburg, and through another scientific peculiarity, the frequency stayed open to the main computer. Simply put, Andy and I were able to communicate even though we were no longer in the same time period. Andy and his dad figured that the transporter opened a wormhole or something between Gettysburg and the laboratory through which the radio waves traveled. The wormhole closes again when the time traveler returns.

"So, Dad, do you think that this new version of the program should compensate for the distortion in time we saw with the old version?" Andy asked.

"I think so. There's no way to know for sure until we test it. Mr. Walton, are you ready for another trip?"

Andy's dad never called me Mr. Walton unless I was in trouble. I was still thinking of my last trip and how scary the whole experience was. I was shocked to hear him ask if I were ready to try again! I must have looked it too, because both Mr. Royce and Andy laughed when they saw the expression on my face. I smiled when I realized that he was kidding. It was times like this when I wished I could thing of something clever to say!

"Actually, let's send this," Mr. Royce said, as he picked up a wrench from his toolbox and placed it on the platform. "Okay, Andy, set the coordinates to the receiver platform and initiate transport."

"Initiating…now!" said Andy. The sensor field net, located above the starting platform, started to vibrate and gave off a low but distinct hum. After a few seconds, the hum seemed to grow into a visible energy field that filled the space between the netting and the surface of the platform. The appearance was similar to an eerie, green fog. After few seconds more, when the wrench was completely obscured by the fog, the process reversed. When the humming and the fog faded away, the platform was empty.

"The wrench is gone!" I shouted.

"Yes. The disintegration part is complete," Mr. Royce said. "The wrench has been broken down at the molecular level. As it was deconstructed, the molecular pattern was stored in the computer data banks. Next, it should reintegrate on the receiving platform."

As if on cue, an energy beam erupted between two posts mounted by the computer operator terminal. The beam curved until it formed a ring encompassing the posts. The ring grew thicker and appeared to fly off the top off the posts. Instantly it was gone. I turned from where the ring dissipated and saw Mr. Royce staring at the receiving platform. Andy was looking at the computer terminal. I didn't want to sound dumb, but I wanted to know what happened.

"Did it work?" I asked, looking at Andy's dad.

"Something went wrong," Mr. Royce answered. "It should have rematerialized on the platform by now."

"The pattern was transferred from the data banks," Andy said. "It must have gone somewhere. This is the same thing that happened when you were transported to Gettysburg, Mark."

"Well, at least the wrench won't end up with a headache like I had! Is it safe to assume that it has been lost in time?"

Andy's dad answered, "Well, one of two things happened. It has either been lost in time, or it failed to reintegrate. If it's lost in time, which I hope is the case, then it should return to the starting platform tomorrow. Otherwise, it may be back to the drawing board. At any rate, our experiment is over for today. All we can do is wait and see."

"That's the part Dad hates most," said Andy.

"I can understand why," I answered. "To have to wait a whole day for the results of an experiment must be frustrating."

"Actually," Andy's dad began, "I can use the time to review the program. I'll work on the premise that the wrench moved through time again and see if I've missed anything. That's the way it is with science. New products rarely work on the first or second attempts. Sometimes the process takes hundreds of trials, and years, to work out all the bugs. Anyway, why don't you kids go have some fun; I'll see what I can do about shortening the test period."

"Okay, but tell us when you're ready to test it again," Andy said.

"Deal," Mr. Royce replied as Andy and I ran out the side door and into the yard.

If anyone could figure this thing out, it was Mr. Royce. It's not an exaggeration to say that he is a genius. He graduated at the top of his class from the Massachusetts Institute of Technology with a doctorate degree in physics. He runs an engineering group for Bell Labs–the company that invented the transistor and other technological miracles–but he always finds time to work on his own projects at home. He does this for fun, and I sincerely hope that I find a career that gives me the same sense of enjoyment that Andy's dad gets from his.

"I can't believe it will take years to get this thing to work," I said.

"Dad didn't say that. He said that *sometimes* it takes years to work out the problems of new inventions. Look at Edison and all the time he put in to invent the light bulb, and he didn't have to wait a whole day to see if it worked. I think this thing is close, but Dad doesn't want to get his, or *our*, hopes up."

Andy was the smartest kid in the eleventh grade, and science and math were his best subjects. Also, we grew up together, so I knew him pretty well. Right now I could tell that he was rolling something over in his mind about the transporter. I considered it my job to get him to talk about it. Sometimes the process of explaining something to me made him think the problem through more thoroughly, and most of the time, all I had to do was ask.

"Okay, you're holding back. What did you see when you were running the station?"

"You noticed, huh?" Andy answered.

"Kinda hard not to," I said. "Why didn't you say something to your dad?"

"Well, for one thing, I'm not sure what I saw. It happened pretty fast. I was trying to scroll through the program as it ran–which is hard enough to do in itself–and I swear I saw a subroutine that doesn't belong there." Andy wandered over to the backyard bench and sat down. His expression indicated that he was more concerned than confused. I sat down next to him, waited a minute or so, and pressed on.

"Okay, what was it?"

"It looks like a piece of code that actually restarts the program after twenty-four hours. I think it was left over from Dad's earlier experiments and he just missed it." Andy still looked concerned, but now I was getting confused.

"Well, can't you just take it out? Delete the extra code I mean."

"You don't get it do you!" Andy was clearly getting upset. He stood up, walked about three steps, and then turned around to face me. "It was that *extra code* that brought you back from Gettysburg. If that wasn't in the program, you would have been stuck in the past, and I would have sent you there!"

So that was it! Andy was still feeling badly about what happened. Actually, in spite of all the excitement, we never talked about it very much. I couldn't believe that Andy thought *I* was holding it against him. Heck, back then I was just as excited to try it as he was. If he was still blaming himself for the accident, then I had to knock some sense into him. I figured I'd try humor first.

"That's not technically true. Actually, I'd be long dead by now."

"Oh, that makes me feel *much* better!" Humor didn't work so I tried logic.

"There's still something about that whole episode that we never discussed. It's entirely possible that I was *supposed* to go back. That by telling the general what his enemy was about to do, he was able to prepare properly and win a great victory!"

"We don't know that for sure! We don't know if the Union won because of your meeting with the generals or in spite of it!" He was right about that and there was no way to prove it. However, there was one undeniable certainty.

"Maybe, but I still had the adventure of a lifetime and so did you! I know I wouldn't trade that for anything. So if you're going to blame yourself for the accident, you have to take credit for the fun we had!" I didn't realize it, but I was standing up and shouting now! That seemed to work because Andy's expression changed and he started to laugh.

"Well, I guess I hadn't thought of it that way. I kind of remember it more as terrifying, though."

"*Of course it was*, but it's fun to think about it now!" We both had a good laugh over that, and I knew that Andy would be all right about it from now on. "So, now that all that unpleasantness is out of the way, why didn't you tell your dad about the extra code?"

"It's still his experiment. Sometimes he needs to concentrate and think things through by himself. I'll look again tomorrow, and if I'm right, and it really is there, I'll tell him then. Come on, the Braves' game is starting."

We're both pretty big baseball fans, but Andy's a fanatic. When the Atlanta Braves are on television, Andy drops whatever he's doing and tunes in. If he ever becomes a surgeon, don't schedule any operations with him in the summer between 7:00 and 10:00 p.m. EDT. He might leave your innards hanging out while he takes a baseball break!

# Chapter 2–An Intruder

The next day I got up early, ate breakfast, and headed over to Andy's. I live three houses away, and over the years I developed the habit of cutting through the yards in between and jumping up on the landing of the back door of his house. When I was little, I could never understand how Andy's mom always knew who it was before she opened the door. It didn't occur to me until I was in high school that I was the only one who rang the back door bell! Today, as I neared Andy's house, I saw someone standing in the back yard peering into the window of the Royces' cellar. He was bent over a little and shading his eyes with his hands to better see inside. At first, I thought it was Andy and I yelled out. It wasn't my friend who looked up but Jeff Belmont. Everyone in the neighborhood calls him Duke except Andy and me. He's your garden-variety bully. Big, tough, and dumb. Emphasis on the dumb. He usually hangs around with a couple of his troll friends. He terrorized the whole neighborhood when we were kids and he was a lot bigger than us, but now that we've grown up some, he isn't so scary. We tolerate him now and even let him play in our Saturday pickup baseball games when he decides to show up, but he isn't the type that we'll ever hang out with.

"Jeffy, what exactly are you doing there, pray tell?" I liked to talk like that to the Duke. A few years ago that would have earned me a pounding, but at nearly six feet and husky, I was as big as the Duke, and I knew he'd never risk a fight with such even odds, especially with no one around to impress. At this moment, he was surprised and stood there looking–well, dumb.

"I say, old chap, were you invited to gaze through yonder window or did you succumb to the temptation to glimpse great men in their natural habitat?" I was in rare form today, and I had a good British accent. The Duke still didn't move so I continued, "Well, out with it, man!"

"Oh stuff it, Walton. I came over here to see what you and your brainy little friend were doing. You two ain't been comin' to the ball field much lately. Whatcha been up to, huh?"

That was true. Normally, we'd never miss the Saturday games, but this past month we'd been spending as much time as possible working with Andy's dad on the transporter. Obviously, I couldn't tell ol' Jeffy that!

"You might say that we have been endeavoring to advance science. Not that any of that could possibly interest you." I *instantly* regretted saying that. I didn't want him, or any of his cronies, wandering about and looking in windows over here every time they got bored. I figured I had an even chance that he wouldn't know what I'd just said. Anyway, Andy came to the back door an instant later.

"Mark, I wish you wouldn't bring such riffraff into the yard. It depresses the scenic vista so." Andy got right into it, too.

"Hey, *Potter*, some day I'll catch you alone and you'll get it good!" Duke said as he turned and stormed off. I wasn't too worried about his threats, and Andy got teased a lot. Lately, some of the kids started calling him Potter after the title character in those books about witches and wizards that became so popular. Actually, I'd never tell *him*, but with his dark and wavy hair, plastic-framed glasses, and slim shape, he *did* look like Harry Potter. Anyway, Duke was gone and that was good, and the day was starting off just fine.

"What was he doing here, anyway?" Andy asked.

"Jeffy misses us, Potter. He says the baseball games just aren't the same without our magnificent presence."

Andy groaned, "I think I'm going to be sick."

"Really, though, he noticed that we haven't been to the games, and I think he was snooping around. We should keep an eye open; we may not have seen the last of him. Hey, did you look at the program? Were you right about what you saw?"

"Come on in the cellar and see for yourself."

We entered the cellar through the door from the side yard. Andy sat down at the terminal, called up the program, and started scrolling. To me it looked like a lot of gibberish going by on the screen, but after a few seconds, Andy slowed the scrolling down and stopped at one line.

"See! Here it is! A *timer* subroutine has been inserted." He scrolled down a few more lines. "And here is the interval. Twenty-four. It must be in hours, and when it times out, the program moves to execute…" more scrolling, "this subroutine…here. A call back. The space / time wormhole isn't collapsing. After twenty-four hours, the object–you, the cat, or the wrench–is being *called* back!"

I didn't understand any of what I just saw, but I nodded my head anyway.

"See, programming is often done in modules, and if a module will function standing alone, it's easier to test. I'm sure Dad programmed this timer but didn't realize that he left it embedded into the module that he was testing. The tests we've done so far mean that at least the call back module works…"

"*And* it means we can change the recall time to anything we want. A week, a year, anything." I added, feeling very excited. "Imagine what it would be like to spend a week, or a month, at Gettysburg–or some other cool, past event!"

"*Ooookaay*, but we're getting ahead of ourselves a little don't you think. We *are* trying to make a transporter that doesn't move objects through time at all, *remember*?" Andy was being the reasonable one this time. It was a switch. I was usually the designated reality check.

"I guess that's true, but we can also reduce the call back time to a few minutes, and we won't have to wait all day between tests if the object gets displaced in time again, right?" I countered, trying my best to sound scientific. Andy liked that idea.

"Hey, that's right! When Dad hears this we'll be heroes! We can run experiments in a fraction of the time it took before! Heck, we could run several in an afternoon!" Andy was working himself into a scientific and mathematical frenzy. The last time this happened he got me excited too, and I ended up in Gettysburg in 1863! I wasn't worried about that happening again, but I was getting a little scared about the direction that this line of thinking could take us, and I made sure that I let Andy know it.

"So who's jumping the gun now?" I asked. "We can't do anything until your dad gets home from work. Besides, yesterday's experiment is still running, remember?"

"Okay, okay! I know we can't do anything now, but it wouldn't hurt to look the program over a little." I relented because I knew he wouldn't be able to think of anything else until his curiosity was satisfied, and this would keep him occupied for a while anyway.

I spent the next few minutes looking over his shoulder at the computer code that was scrolling on the screen. I didn't know where Andy learned to read all that. Our computer work in school never reached that level of sophistication. I figured that maybe his dad taught him, or more likely, his dad told him about it, and he taught himself.

I was amazed at some of the stuff that he learned to do overnight! In elementary school, way back when, we spent lunch period watching a couple of the teachers play chess. I wasn't paying much attention because, quite frankly, the whole thing bored me to death. Andy, on the other hand, was watching with great interest. When the game ended, he very matter-of-factly told the winning teacher that he would play him the next day. The man laughed, and I knew that he didn't take Andy seriously. I smiled too, because I knew Andy had never learned chess. On the way home from school, I asked him why he challenged a teacher to a game he didn't even know how to play. He told me that he liked contests of strategy, and all he had to do was learn how the pieces moved. He also said that he guessed that that teacher was probably the best in the school, and even if he lost, he'd learn more about the game by playing against him than anyone else. At the time, I figured all my friend was going to do was embarrass himself in front of everyone.

By the next day, most of our class had heard about Andy's challenge, including our teacher, Miss Ayer. At the start of lunch break, he ran down to the teacher's classroom with most of us in tow. Even Miss Ayer came along. When we reached the teacher's room, it was apparent that he hadn't expected Andy to show up, and he was setting up for a rematch with his opponent from the previous day. When he saw Andy standing there, he apologized to his friend and invited Andy to sit down. The class gathered around the players and the match was on. It seemed to last forever, but none of us left. Finally, Andy made his last move and announced "checkmate" to his opponent! All the kids gasped! Miss Ayer started to giggle and quickly covered her mouth with her hand.

The teacher looked up with a distinct smile on his face and asked Miss Ayer what she found so amusing. Miss Ayer said that she had an idea that something like this might happen, and that she wasn't going to miss it. He extended his hand to Andy and gave our classmate a hearty handshake. He asked him his name, and when Andy replied, the teacher told my friend that he expected to be hearing of young Mr. Royce in the future. Andy thanked him for the match and led us all out the door.

When I asked Andy how he did it, how he learned chess over night and then beat the teacher, he told me that learning the moves was easy. At first, when the match started, he played cautiously. He'd move a piece and make sure that it wasn't going to get attacked from anywhere. Soon he was able to look two or three moves ahead. By the middle of the match, it was four or five. Once he got there, he was able to keep the teacher occupied at one end of the board while he attacked from the other. I knew after that day, that my friend wasn't your average, run-of-the-mill kid. I eventually learned chess, and I can *still* only see two or three moves ahead. Needless to say, I've never beaten Andy, although I do fairly well with my other friends. He's just at a whole different level. As I said, it was amazing what Andy could teach himself.

I realized that I had been daydreaming and that Andy had stopped scrolling and was staring intently at one section of code. "Find something interesting, did you?" I asked. No answer. "Heellooo, what are you looking at?" A little louder this time, "Hey Andy, look outside there's a blizzard going on!" A neat trick for August!

"You say something, Mark?" Andy spoke at last.

"I asked if you *found* anything," I repeated.

"I don't know, maybe. It's going to take a while to decipher, though."

"That's okay. I have to go. My sister's getting back from day camp, and I have to keep an eye on her till my mom or dad gets home. I'll come back after supper."

"Okay, Dad'll be home by then. I've got a few questions about this code, too. Be back by 7:30, that's when the wrench should return."

I left Andy's house and made it home minutes before my sister. That was close, but after our fun with the Duke, I was feeling good. I just had a sense that things were going to go my way all day.

# Chapter 3—Return Of The Intruder

My sister and I ate lunch and played in the yard most of the afternoon. Katie is twelve and starting to get interesting. She'd follow me everywhere if she could, and I have to admit that it's a pretty good feeling having someone around who looks up to you all the time. I do get tired of hearing her play the latest teenybopper-band CDs, but I guess she's just being normal. On the occasional Saturday, she and her friends will come down to the park to watch us play baseball. They're mostly occupied with giggling and pointing, but it cracks me up just the same. When Andy comes over, she never leaves the room, or the yard, or wherever he is. I think she has a crush on him, but I've never teased her about it. Andy, of course, is oblivious to the whole thing.

After supper I was anxious to get back over to Andy's to see how yesterday's experiment turned out. Also, Mr. Royce and Andy probably had some theories about what to try for the next experiment. I told Mom and Dad I was leaving and headed out the back door. It was dusk on a perfect summer night. I was a half-dozen steps from my back door when I saw three figures sneaking around Andy's yard. The Duke and his cronies! They were approaching the door to Andy's cellar. The lights were on, so I knew that neither Andy nor his dad could see out. I decided to see if I could find out what these hoodlums were up to, so I moved in slowly and hid behind some bushes positioned directly behind the cellar door. The Duke and his buddies were crowding the window, but they were crouched down, and I could still see in above them. I was a good forty feet away, so I couldn't make out what they were watching, but at precisely 7:30 p.m., the generator kicked on, and I saw the green glow through the window. The wrench had returned! At that moment, the Duke and his trolls jumped back, and I started howling and shaking the bushes at the same time. Instantly all three bolted from the yard as fast as their frightened legs could carry them! I had to bite my lip to keep from bursting into noisy laughter and giving my position away. In three seconds, they were out of sight!

I knocked on the cellar door, heard Andy and his dad yell, and went inside. Mr. Royce was holding the wrench, and Andy was looking over the computer monitor.

"I see that the wrench returned!" I said. "I saw the glow from outside."

"Yup, right on schedule," Mr. Royce replied. "That was some nice work that you and Andy did this morning. I wrote that timer subroutine at the earliest stages of the project, and quite frankly, I forgot all about it. I must have included it when I cut and pasted that section of programming code."

Andy added, "We're going to take your suggestion and leave the timer in the program. We can shorten the call back interval to fifteen minutes and get results faster."

"That sounds great," I said, "but have you figured out what to try next? I mean did you find anything in the program that might help."

"No, Mark, I didn't find anything and neither did Dad."

"I need to rethink the whole premise of inter-dimensional travel. The new model will need to include the added dimension of time as well as space. I'm afraid this is going to take quite a while, maybe the rest of the summer or more," Andy's dad said. I don't know who was more disappointed, Mr. Royce or us.

"Is there anything Andy and I can do to speed up the process?" I asked. I couldn't believe that we were shutdown cold over this.

"There really isn't right now, Mark. Thanks for the offer but all the calculations have been based on the three *spatial* dimensions–length, width, and height. I have to add a fourth, *time*, into the model now. That complicates the design significantly. If it's any consolation, the upside is that the finished device will have the capability to control travel through both time and space. However, the world may not be ready for that just yet. Don't worry; I'll let you guys know when it's time to resume the experimental phase. I'll bet Christopher is happy, anyway."

Christopher is the cat's name and upon hearing it, he gave a loud meow and padded over to his dish. Mr. Royce gave him some dry food and headed upstairs. Andy and I sat on the bench with our heads hanging. This was the kind of disappointment you felt when you were just about to go to Disney World and your vacation plans were canceled at the last minute. Neither one of us wanted to talk, but I finally broke the silence.

"The Duke and his scumbags were here again. They were looking in the window when the wrench was called back."

"You mean they saw the whole thing?" Andy sounded a lot more concerned than I would have figured.

"Well, I know they saw the usual green glow, but that was about it. I started howling from the bushes. It freaked them out, and they ran like crazy!" I started to laugh as I thought about it again. Andy got into it, too. The day that started out with so much promise and ended with a major disappointment at least included some fun moments.

# Chapter 4—The World Turned Sideways!

It was back to baseball for Andy and me since our part in the development of the time machine–there was really no reason to call it anything else now–was on hold. I have to admit that I really missed the game. That first trip back on the field was a rush. My timing was off, and my fielding was clearly rusty, but I expected that. Just to swing the bat and throw the ball again felt great. It also helped to clear my head about the events of the last few weeks. I didn't even mind Katie and her friends watching and giggling.

Andy, on the other hand, was distracted. He was playing on the same field as the rest of us, but it was clear that his head was somewhere else. I knew he was still locked in on the experiment. I only hoped that he wouldn't do anything crazy until he got over it.

The Duke was back on the field, too. He seemed a little quieter since our meeting in Andy's backyard, but I still didn't trust him. Fortunately, we hadn't seen him or his followers sneaking around the cellar lately. I figured that they were still recovering from the scare they got.

After the game, Andy and I hung around to practice our throwing. We didn't play long, but by the time we headed for home, the field was empty. We play on the Thayer Academy field, which is about a half-mile from our homes. We both attend Braintree High School, which is about the same distance, but for some reason, we've always played on the academy grounds. I guess old habits are hard to break. It takes about fifteen minutes to walk from the field to our houses over beautifully treed, suburban roads. It may not be stylish to like your hometown, but I can think of worse places to grow up. Most of the walk is flat, but our road, Oak Hill Road, is a fairly steep, uphill grade. I live about four houses up on the left in a raised ranch. Andy lives three houses further up in a similar house with a basement door that opens to the side yard. As we turned into my backyard, the door to his basement was plainly visible. I noticed it first. The door was open. "I didn't think your dad was home today. Is he working on the time machine?" I asked, as I put my glove and ball down on the patio. It wasn't unusual for Mr. Royce to leave the cellar door open when he was in there. He liked to wander out to the yard and pace while he thought. Andy did the same thing, especially on a beautiful, sunny, summer day like this.

"No, he's at work. He put some effort in last night, but he left at his usual time this morning," Andy replied.

"Your mom, maybe?" I asked.

"Maybe, but she doesn't go into the cellar often. That's how we got away with your trip to Gettysburg, remember?" I remembered. I was gone for twenty-four hours, and Andy was in the cellar nearly the whole time, but his mom never found out. Then Andy added, "We'd better go check it out." At that we started walking.

By the time we reached his side yard, we heard the generator start. Then a noise came from inside the cellar. It was dark in there, so neither of us could see anything, but we both knew what we were hearing–the whine of the time machine as it powered up. We both broke into sprints and made it inside just as the green glow was beginning to fade. Someone had activated the time machine! But *who*? And *why* wasn't he here? *Or* did he send himself off somewhere? Andy and I both looked at each other, then at the platform, then at each other again. We were totally puzzled! I spoke first, "You don't think the cat stepped on the keyboard or something, do you?"

"I don't know," Andy said. Just then, Christopher the cat meowed as he sprang out from under the bench by the computer. It was apparent that he'd been hiding from something or someone.

"Who then?" I asked. Andy didn't respond. He ran up the stairs and yelled "MOM" when he reached the door at the top. No answer. Also, the door seemed to be jammed from the other side.

"That's strange," Andy said. "The door isn't locked, but it won't open. It's almost as if something big and solid is pressing up against it. MOM!" Andy yelled again.

I don't know what made me do it, but I started walking back outside. "Well, somebody had to start this thing," I said, as I stepped into the side yard. It took a moment for my eyes to readjust to the light. As my vision began to clear, and I saw my surroundings, I was nearly overcome by a powerful sense of dread! My jaw dropped open, and my mouth dried out! I could feel my heart start to pound, and I was profoundly dizzy. I was having a full-blown anxiety attack. Andy's yard was gone! I was standing in the middle of woods! I turned to look at the house and saw a dilapidated barn instead! The foundation and the two sides were made of fieldstone. One side was right against the door that Andy was trying to open. That explained the problem he was having. The back of the barn, the part that used to be the back of Andy's house, was now old, worn, barn boards. I could see daylight through the gaping holes in some of the vertical slats. Apparently the roof wasn't in much better condition. I looked into the direction of my house. Nothing but woods. No houses, no manicured little lawns, no swing sets or patios. Nothing had ever been built here!

I stumbled back into the cellar. Andy was studying the computer screen. He looked up when he saw me approach. "What happened to you? You look like a walking zombie!" he said. I didn't reply. I couldn't; I was in shock! I turned when I got to the bench by the computer terminal and sat down. Andy kept looking at the screen. "The coordinates are here, but I can't find the geographical location that they represent. The look-up program only works one way. You can enter a location and get the coordinates, but you can't enter coordinates and retrieve a location. Also, I can't tell what–if anything–was transported"

"Not what," I said softly. I didn't realize it, but I was speaking in monosyllables. I was clearly stunned.

"What did you say?" Andy asked.

"Not what," I repeated. "Who. Or is it whom?" I giggled incoherently.

"You think a person transported himself somewhere?" he asked.

"I'm sure," I said. "Go look outside." Andy looked at me with a studied expression. I returned a blank stare. All I could do was point through the doorway to the outside. Andy rose and moved in that direction. He stopped about two steps into the yard. I could tell the moment that the view registered in his mind because that's when he began screaming.

"WHAT THE H—L IS GOING ON!" Andy never swore. He considered profanity an indication of a deficient vocabulary, but in this case, there really were no words sufficient to describe the scene. His shouting, however, served to wake me up! I ran out the cellar door, grabbed him, and covered his mouth to shut him up. Then I dragged him back inside. He was flailing about so I was grateful for my size advantage, and I managed to wrestle him to the ground. My next step was to talk him back into sanity. His eyes were wild, and I knew that this might not be an easy task.

"*Look*, something's happened! We both know that, but we need you *clear-headed*!" I said firmly. "We *can't be sure* what it's like out there. Something has happened, and I've got to figure the time machine had something to do with this. Let's not call attention to ourselves until we get the lay of the land! Okay?"

Andy nodded. He'd stopped struggling and his eyes were focused. I knew he'd be all right now, so I let him go.

"Sorry about that; I freaked out," he said.

"So did I. I was just quieter about it than you were," I answered. We both managed thin smiles and realized that we had some investigating to do.

# Chapter 5—Discovery Of A New Past

It was very apparent that something had happened after the time machine was activated this time. None of our recent experiments had resulted in even the slightest observable change in our surroundings. Mr. Royce had transported wrenches, cats, and other objects only to have them return unaltered after the call back module kicked in. When *I* went back to Gettysburg, however, I gave some information about Thomas Edison to Captain Southbridge and two other men in the Union army. My new friends took full advantage of their peek into the future, and we now buy power from the Edison–Southbridge Electric Company! It was a very stupid and risky thing for me to do, and we were lucky that no other significant changes resulted. I learned my lesson and vowed never to mess with the past again if the situation ever came up.

But something *had* happened! The time machine was activated, and now some strange, new world was all around us. This was our dilemma. Did someone use the machine, go into the past, and alter history? What would be the motive? Did *we* somehow change location? That had never happened before. The magnitude of all this was impossible to determine from Andy's yard, but it was information that we had to have. "Could we have moved?" I asked when Andy returned to the computer screen.

"No," Andy answered. "Physically, we're in the same place. Didn't you notice the tree out back?"

I hadn't, so I looked outside again. Andy was right. The old maple that we'd been climbing for years was there. Other, smaller trees that I hadn't seen before surrounded it, but there was no mistaking that one. Just seeing it made me feel better somehow.

"Any ideas?" I asked.

"I think you were right the first time. This couldn't have happened by itself; *someone* had to cause this. I suspect that someone activated the time machine and traveled back in time. By some action, they altered the historical timeline. I can't say for sure that is what happened, but I can't see an alternative."

Something was still bothering me, so I kept at it. "The neighborhood is missing, is it possible that we are in a different time as well? A time before the houses were built?"

"No, we are still in the twenty-first century. Something happened to cause this world to evolve differently. Apparently in such a way that our neighborhood was never built."

"I do have one very good question for you."

"And that is?" Andy returned.

"Why are *we* still here? Why didn't *we* change, or disappear, or just become part of this new world?"

"Good question. I don't know. The only thing that I can think of is that this immediate area," Andy spread his arms and gestured toward the walls of the cellar, "was somehow insulated from any changes resulting from alterations of the timeline. We must have been close enough to the electrical field that we were insulated, too. The same goes for the equipment. Fortunately, the generator is physically connected by the wiring, or that may have been gone."

"And if we were two seconds later…?"

"Then we would have been part of this new world, too," Andy finished.

"Or never been born," I added with a shudder.

"Unfortunately, that would have been a very likely scenario."

"Well, at least we have the time machine. Is it working?" I asked.

"I think so. We never changed the timer, so within twenty-four hours, if someone went back in time, they'll be called back. We can either sit here and wait until then, or do a little looking around on our own. I have the coordinates of our time traveler's destination, maybe we can find out something from that," Andy suggested.

"Sounds fine to me. Let's see if there's anything out there. Do you have a compass? These woods may go on for some time."

"I *did* have one, but it was in my room. We're on our own now." And with that we both headed off. Our route took us in the direction of South Braintree square, which was about a mile away. That pathway would lead us through the school grounds where we were playing baseball earlier that day. I don't know what Andy was thinking, but I couldn't help worrying about my sister and family. I don't think fifteen minutes had passed since we first entered the cellar in the wake of the time traveler, but it seemed like a lifetime. Even if we did find out what happened, what could we do to fix everything? Or, *should* we do anything to change it?

After about twenty minutes of picking our way through the woods, we came to a clearing. Andy reacted first. "Hey, Thayer Academy's still here!" he exclaimed. I was amazed, but the school was, in fact, still there. The additional buildings, those added over the passed forty years or so, were gone, but the original stone structure was standing tall. A groundskeeper was mowing the infield of the track loop. It was a very comforting site to see. At least now we knew that we weren't the only two people left in the world!

We continued up to the back of the school, and except for the missing buildings, everything looked the same. When we came around the side of the main structure, I looked over the field to my right. It was then that I noticed something very different. Something almost tragic–there was *no* baseball field!

"The field looks a little different, doesn't it, Andy?" I asked.

"Actually, it looks exactly the same to me. I wouldn't have expected that–hey, *where's the baseball field?*"

"I don't know, but let's keep going. The main building is here and that's something. Let's head into town and see what we can find out." We walked out onto the lawn at the front of the school. The main road looked nearly the same as before, but traffic seemed very light. It could have been my imagination, though. The cars were certainly strange looking. They were small and rounded, like the old Volkswagen Beetle, except older and shabby looking. I turned around and spied the front of the school building. Big block letters read: "HORATIO NELSON REGIONAL SECONDARY SCHOOL." This morning it had read "THAYER ACADEMY." Now *that* was a major change. I tapped Andy on the shoulder. "Hey, look at that," I said as I pointed to the school name.

"Ha! Well at least it's in English. We'll still be able to read books and road signs. It also explains that!" Andy pointed to the flagpole. It wasn't the Stars and Stripes that was flying high and waving free but the British Union Jack! At that, we sat on the stone wall by the sidewalk to digest what we had learned.

"I say there, old chap, it seems that we're no longer in the United States," I started, trying to make light of a situation that was growing weirder by the minute.

"Quite so. Apparently the colonies must still be the colonies, my good man," Andy replied. We knew this was serious, but I think we both felt relieved. After all, we could have found ourselves in some kind of modern Mongol empire, or the American Soviet Socialist Republic.

"Let's approach this as a scientific problem," Andy went on. "Step one–form a hypothesis. What do we know for sure?"

I could always count on Andy to take the technical route. I didn't have any better ideas, so I played along. "What we knew as the United States is now part of the British Empire. We're sure of that by the flag," I said.

"That's fair, and it seems that they don't play baseball here. They don't play it in England either," Andy continued.

"Also, the school name. It seems reasonable that a high school would be named after a British hero," I added. Back in junior high school, our history teacher told us the story of Admiral Horatio Nelson and Britain's great naval victory at the Battle of Trafalgar. That battle ended any hope that the French and Spanish navies would ever mount a serious threat to British sea supremacy during the Napoleonic Wars.

"Right. Now thinking about our own past, what could have happened that may have caused this?"

"The American Revolution was never fought!" I jumped in. Andy was baiting me a little, but I didn't mind. I knew that he loved the *process* of discovery almost as much as the discovery itself. Plus, working on a puzzle was a good way to keep us focused on the action at hand rather worrying about what may have happened to our families.

"Or, that it was fought and lost!" Andy said. "That's our hypothesis. That the American Revolution was either avoided or lost by the Americans."

"That's really two hypotheses. I think that's invalid." I took this opportunity to chide Andy about the scientific process. He didn't seem to mind.

"Okay, but we'll test them both at once. Step two–test the hypothesis. Let's find a library and look up some history." With that, Andy was up and moving.

"And where is the library?" I asked.

"Well, the school's closed, so let's see if the library downtown is still there."

As we walked along, we pointed out the areas that had changed. I couldn't help but notice that the town seemed slow. Well, not slow exactly, more like the pace was typical of a Saturday morning rather than a weekday afternoon. Besides the cars, everything looked shabby. The roads were paved, but seemed narrower than I remember. Also, whole blocks of houses, which we knew in our world, just weren't there. I couldn't think of any direct explanation for this except that the Braintree, Massachusetts of my timeline was clearly more affluent. Neither could Andy and for some reason, we decided not to speculate. Hopefully the library would be there, and we'd get our answers soon enough.

# Chapter 6–Research

Luck was with us and the library *was* still there. Ours was called the Thayer Public Library, and it had been remodeled and enlarged just last year. This was called the Braintree Public Library and it was apparent that it hadn't been improved in many years. Nevertheless, facts were facts and we figured that it would serve our purpose. We stopped short of entering, and I turned to my friend.

"Andy, this may be the first time that we actually meet anyone from this…place." We still hadn't figured out what to call where we were. "Don't you think we should have some plan if they ask us where we came from?"

"I guess you're right. This Braintree is smaller than ours, and for all we know, we may have different accents or something. What do you think?"

"Tell anyone who asks that we're from Fairhaven, New Hampshire–way up north. I have an uncle who used to live up in the north woods, and we'd visit him from time to time. His place was near the Canadian border. Nothing much up there and he didn't even have electricity. The name–Fairhaven–I made up. I really don't remember what it was called, or if it even had a name at all, but at least that way we can't stumble onto someone who may have been there," I answered.

"Fairhaven. I like it. Hopefully we won't need the cover."

The library had an open floor plan with benches and tables grouped in the center and bookshelves around the perimeter. Directly behind the center area was the reference section. The library was nearly empty, but I felt better knowing that we had a plan in case something came up. We attracted a few stares, but it wasn't our accents; it was the way we were dressed! I never considered either of us fashion trendsetters, but the clothes on these people were what our *parents* would wear! This world may still be in the twenty-first century, but I felt like I'd walked into the 1970s. Actually, I decided that I definitely liked the long hair and hip hugger jeans that a group of girls sitting at a table was wearing. I don't think they thought the same about us, though. Three of them stared openly, while the fourth tried desperately, and equally unsuccessfully, to hide behind a book. If she laughed any harder, she was going to need the little girls' room! Pretty soon they were *all* giggling, and I was happy to see that Andy was already moving into the reference section to look for the atlases.

I followed him, but I couldn't resist the urge to glance back at the table. One girl in particular caught my eye. When I turned back around, I nearly walked into Andy. "Find anything?" I asked, even though I knew he hadn't had time to get started.

"Oh, we're through flirting with the locals are we?" he answered with a wry smile. "They're cute, wouldn't you say?" I wouldn't have guessed that he even noticed the little exchange. I instantly wondered if he knew about Katie. If he did, he would be too polite to say anything.

"*Very* cute," I answered. "You know, our situation could be a whole lot worse." I started to scan the area. "Why are you looking in those?" I asked, pointing to the books. "Let's use the computers."

"Boy, you must really be smitten," Andy said. "Take a look around you." I did, and I didn't know how I could have missed it before. No computers! There was a monitor, or rather a television set, in the corner of the reference area, but it had a channel changer that you cranked by hand. Clearly we wouldn't be getting any help from the internet on that thing. I doubted if there even was an internet here. I guess *this* world never had Al Gore!

"Here we go." Andy said, staring down at the map of the eastern seaboard of North America. "The scale is still too large, but we can narrow our search a lot. Look," he let his finger trace a circle that took in New

York, Philadelphia, and Baltimore, "our answer lies somewhere in this area. Let's get the detailed map of Pennsylvania." The library had an excellent reference section, and I quickly found the right book. I opened it to Pennsylvania and handed it to Andy.

"Nope. It's not in Pennsylvania, but it's darn close. See this area here," he traced the irregular line that marked the state's eastern border, "that's the Delaware River." I nodded. I knew that already, but Andy was on a roll. "East of that is New Jersey," he continued. "We need the detailed map of New Jersey."

I had the book out and was already opening it to the correct page by the time Andy looked up. We were very close to answering the key question: Where did the traveler go? I could see that he was getting excited as I handed him the book–opened to the map.

With the index finger on his left hand, Andy traced the line of longitude. With his right hand, he traced the latitude. As his two fingers met, Andy exclaimed, "Trenton! Trenton, New Jersey!" He looked up in triumph and closed the book with a clap. I was smiling as well, happy that we had the answer to our first question, but the sudden "smack" of the book closing startled me. It also startled a middle-aged lady in a conservative business suit, who was reading nearby. Andy lowered his voice. "Now all we have to do is figure out what happened in Trenton that stopped the American Revolution."

"Or finished it," I added.

"Right," Andy answered. Neither of us noticed, but the lady had moved closer and was now listening to our conversation. When we turned to move to the history section, I nearly knocked her over.

"Oh, I'm sorry!" I said. "Are you all right?"

"Oh, yes. Quite," she answered, "but the answer to your query is Washington's defeat at the Battle of Trenton in 1776, of course," she added. This stopped us dead in our tracks.

"*George* Washington?" Andy asked.

"Yes! George Washington the *Rebel*! How old are you boys?" she asked, casting a stern look and clearly meaning it as a reproach. Andy and I looked at each other. We were both puzzled by the question, but neither of us answered. The lady tried again. "Surely, you know *that* much."

I took the plunge this time. "Sixteen," I answered.

"Haven't you had English history? It's required in both middle and secondary schools," she asked.

"Well sure, but we haven't gotten to that part yet. Did you get there yet, Andy?" I asked, trying to look serious and stalling for time. Our second encounter with the townspeople was not going as well as the first.

"No. Not yet. That's why we're doing this school project about the Revolution," he added.

"Rebellion. It's called the American Colonial Rebellion. Where do you boys go to school?" she asked.

"We're from New Hampshire. Fairhaven, New Hampshire, ma'am," I said.

"Well, I see that they at least teach you manners there. I *sincerely* hope they are working on the history curriculum as well. You see, I'm a history teacher in Weymouth, just up the street, so I'm probably a little more critical than most. But as long as you're here, I'll show you some good books on the subject."

"Thank you, we'd appreciate that," Andy put in.

The teacher from Weymouth was as good as her word. Actually, she gave us more reference books than we could possibly read, but she went to great pains to show us the sections on the American Colonial Rebellion in general and the Battle of Trenton in particular. After she left, Andy and I began our research in earnest.

"Here's the Stamp Act in 1765, but no mention of either The Boston Tea Party, or the Boston Massacre. Interesting, huh, since we know that history up until that point hasn't changed," Andy said.

"Look at this," I said as I began to read from the book I was holding:

> *"The Quartering Act of 1774 was instituted to protect the good British subjects of Boston from the lawless Rebels. This was only partially successful since the cancer of rebellion had spread throughout the city. Many Rebel sympathizers were required to house the King's soldiers. In such cases, the red-coated patriotic protectors could expect to be shabbily treated for their efforts to bring order to the city. Extraordinary patience and tolerance by the King's colonial representatives kept the door of compromise open despite the continued refusal of the Rebels to comply with even the most reasonable demands. Armed conflict was forced upon the Crown when the rebellious faction fired on troops at Bunker Hill as they attempted to restore order to the besieged city. Little did they know that that signal act would doom their cause."*

"I think I'm going to puke," I said.

"Hey, the winners write the history books," Andy shrugged. "That explains why there's no mention of Tea Parties and Massacres. It's likely that nothing was ever preserved about those little episodes." Andy seemed to be taking this in stride. He expected this to happen. I wasn't prepared to read about my country's past in such sour references. I thought back to our history books. Did we vilify the British and glorify the Rebels? I considered Longfellow's poem, *Paul Revere's Ride*, the fact that the Boston Tea Party and the Boston Massacre are historical beacons in the fight for freedom to us, and how we refer to the Rebels as Patriots. I realized, of course, that I had answered my own question. Yes, in our timeline, the American Revolution was won, and the United States was formed. *We* wrote the history, and the British were the villains while the American Patriots were the heroes. I still wasn't satisfied, and I stood up.

"Where are you going?" Andy asked.

"To test a theory," I replied and marched over to the table of girls. They were still there talking quietly amongst themselves but went silent as I approached. The giggler began to leaf through the magazine she was holding. The others stared at me with expressions ranging from mild amusement to genuine shock. This might be fun, I thought.

"Hi, my name is Mark," I began. "My friend and I have to do a report this summer on the American Revolu…er, American Colonial Rebellion. Have you heard of it?"

"Yeeesss, I think everyone has heard about that," the girl, who had caught my eye earlier, answered. She was wearing a light pink, summer blouse, and she had long, soft, blond hair that flowed over her shoulders. Her bright eyes were quizzical behind round lenses, and I thought that I caught a slight smile at the edges of her mouth. I was becoming distracted, as I began to truly regret missing the 1970s. Her friend, the giggler, started up again, and that shook me back to reality.

"How about the Battle of Trenton?" I asked. My voice cracked a little. I hoped she…er…they didn't notice.

"That ended the Rebellion, if that's what you're looking for," she answered. Beautiful and smart, too. Okay, stay focused, Mark, I thought to myself

"How about the Boston Massacre, or the Boston Tea Party?" This was the part I was really looking forward to.

"No. Never heard of those. Were they during the Rebellion?" she asked.

"Just before it actually, but they were two of the primary events that started it."

"Oh, maybe you can tell me about it some time," she said. Several of the girls were standing up and clearly preparing to leave. "We're going to the plaza now. Maybe we'll see you there."

"The South Shore Plaza?" I asked. That was a major hangout in my timeline as well. At least that was still here.

She laughed at that. "It's the only plaza around here that I know of. Oh, I'm Amy. 'Bye now." And as quickly as that they were gone. But I had my answer. Andy was right. The winners write the history books.

When I returned, Andy was sitting in a booth totally absorbed in some history text. I picked up a book, found another booth nearby, and started leafing though it. My mind kept wandering back to Amy, and I couldn't concentrate on what I was reading. Andy was right; I was smitten, but this was no time get mushy. I continued this way for about an hour and decided to see what Andy had found out. I walked back over to the booth where he was sitting.

He looked up at me with an expression of pure shock. "This is incredible," was all he managed to say.

"What?" I asked. "Did you find something interesting?"

"Interesting isn't the word for it! I'm almost up to the present. We wouldn't recognize much about the past. Whew…" Andy closed the book and sat back.

"I'll bet the Civil War wasn't fought," I said.

"Well, you're right about that," Andy replied. "But wait till you hear this!"

"What?" My curiosity was up now! Andy was pale, and his eyes were sort of glazed over.

"World War II is *still* going on!"

# Chapter 7—The Orwellian World

"Come on, let's go outside. I need some air, and I'll fill you in," Andy said as he got up to leave. We had nearly reached the library door when I glanced at a newspaper that was lying on the table. It was dated today and the headline read: "*NAZI EUROPE RUMORED TO BE TESTING A SUPER BOMB!*" Now *that* was a frightening thought. I could only assume that they meant the atomic bomb. I pointed to the table to show Andy. He shook his head and moaned a quiet, "Oh, no." We left the library and walked across the street to a park called French's Common. We played ball here too, but a soccer field was where the baseball diamond used to be. We moved to the stands at the edge of the grass and sat down. I looked up and saw a jet fly overhead. It looked like a military jet, but the town itself showed no outward signs of a war going on.

"Maybe you should start at the beginning," I said. "Did you find out what happened at Trenton?"

"I think so," he began. "Remember the battle in our timeline? General Washington crossed the Delaware River on Christmas night and attacked the Hessians in Trenton the morning after."

I thought about that. The British purchased troops from princes of the various German principalities. The princes received a kind of lease fee for the use of their soldiers. Most came from the region known as Hesse-Cassel and were called Hessians. The term became a catch all for any mercenary troops used by the British during the Revolution. They were professional soldiers, well trained and disciplined. In a conventional battle, General Washington felt that his troops of half-starved farmers, fisherman, and artisans would fare poorly against these well-equipped and expertly prepared adversaries. As a result, Washington planned the attack to achieve the best chance of surprise.

"Sure, he surprised them totally and bagged the whole lot," I answered.

"Well, in *this* timeline the Hessians were waiting for them and utterly *destroyed* the Americans. The Continentals panicked, and the rout was complete. Washington was captured, tried for treason, and hung along with most of the leaders of the Rebellion. Without Washington, the American Revolution was *over.* Lost. No constitution, no baseball, hot dogs, apple pie or Chevrolets."

"So, someone went back and warned the Hessians that Washington was coming," I said.

"That would be my guess," Andy replied.

"The evidence seems to point in that direction more and more."

"That it does."

"Who would do that?" I asked.

"I have no idea. It doesn't make any sense," Andy said.

"What happened next?"

"The French still had their revolution, and Napoleon ended up emperor, and the Napoleonic Wars were fought and won by the British and their allies the same as in our timeline. After Napoleon was defeated, the British scooped up the rest of France's holdings in North America. That was the equivalent of President Jefferson's Louisiana Purchase. At least the land that was ceded was the same. From what I could tell, all the land west of that–Texas, New Mexico, Arizona, Nevada, and California–is *still* part of Mexico.

"The war cost so much, that taxes in the colonies were raised to record levels to pay the crown. Taxes were based on property values. Slaves were considered valuable property and taxed accordingly. The plantation owners found that it was more economical to free their slaves and hire them back at low wages. That way, they avoided the taxes and still got the labor. Many of the freed slaves moved west and settled onto their own farms. No slaves, no constitutional crisis with the North, and…"

"No Civil War." I finished for him.

"Right. But some changes didn't work out so well. The Indian Wars seemed just as brutal with approximately the same result. Immigration wasn't encouraged during the latter half of the 1800s and the population of British North America–as this is called, by the way–stayed fairly low. At least as compared to what it is in our timeline. Also, Mother England maintained a colonial economy here–that is, it used North America mainly for raw materials and kept the bulk of the factories at home. So now you have a reduced population and little manufacturing, and even though British North America combines the land area of what we know as Canada and most of the United States, it had little industrial power by 1900."

I was amazed at how much Andy learned after spending so little time reading. It would have taken me a week to learn that much, but I understood what he was getting at. A weak British North America was a bad omen for freedom in the twentieth century. In our timeline, the 1900s were known as the American Century for reasons that were clear. The industrial and military might of the United States played a leading roll in defeating the enemies of freedom. This was particularly true of Fascist Italy, Nazi Germany, and Imperial Japan in the Second World War. Without that strength, it appeared that Fascism gained a foothold, and after seeing that headline in the newspaper, it could be on the verge of global domination.

"So the Allies win the First World War but it took longer, and the Nazis rose up anyway." I was guessing, but I wanted to get in on the action.

"Pretty much. The Soviet overthrow of Czarist Russia still happened, and Hitler's Nazis controlled Germany by the mid 1930s. When World War II started, England and France were as unprepared as they were in our timeline. France and the rest of the European mainland were overrun. The

Soviet Union lost most of the Ukraine, and England held. Without the United States, though, the sides fought to a stalemate. No end in sight. The fighting goes on, but nothing was…is ever resolved."

A simple "Wow," was all I could muster. Then, "What happened to Japan?"

"More of the same. Right now they're bogged down in China, Southeast Asia, and Northern Australia. They keep fighting, too. There's no fighting in either North or South America–at least not yet."

"So what does the world look like?" I asked, although I was afraid to hear the answer.

"Well, England and British North America are on one side. The British are holding off the Nazis in North Africa, and they're helping the Australians fight Japan. The Soviet Union is still intact and has stopped the Nazis somewhere in the Ukraine. The Soviets gain ground in the winter and lose it back in the summer. Japan has an armed border on the Soviet eastern front. The rest of Japan I told you about. Also, I look around this place and from the photographs my dad has, I'd guess this world is about a quarter of a century behind–technologically speaking."

This was a lot to swallow at once. Imagine a world at war all the time–a continuous grinding of men and machinery in some macabre mill! I thought about Amy and her friends living with this constantly. I'm sure the men from British North America made regular tours of duty fighting at the front. For everyone, this was a regular way of life. I wasn't saying anything. I was lost in my own thoughts when Andy's voice broke through.

"All that may be about to change, now. If that headline is true, and the Nazis develop the atomic bomb, they'll end the war quickly. Hey, Mark, how do you feel about a Nazi world?" Andy asked.

"Dude, that's too horrible to imagine," I answered.

"And that's our incentive to fix this mess," Andy returned. He got no argument from me.

# Chapter 8—Coins To Pounds

The names were a little different, but this was similar to the world that George Orwell wrote about in his book *1984*. It was funny because 1984 seems so long ago. When I read his book in school last year, I remember thinking how glad I was that the world didn't turn out that way. Now, in this timeline, we found that the Battle of Trenton was lost in 1776, and that made George Orwell's prediction of totalitarian states and a continuous world war come true. I wondered what else was bubbling under the surface of a society that's been fighting for over half a century. That explained why cars were small and few, and the whole town looked as though it were in need of a complete overhaul. Basics would be in short supply. Such things as gasoline, cloth, bread, and shoes would be selling at a premium or rationed.

"Let's go back to the lab," Andy said. "We need to plan the next trip in the time machine to set the timeline back to its proper course. I think there's another transmitter around that we can use, but I'll have to find it."

"That sounds fine, but I could go for some food. It's late afternoon and we skipped lunch."

"Now that you mention it, I'm hungry, too. I guess I didn't think of it in all the excitement."

That surprised me. The one thing that was a constant in any world was Andy's appetite. He was slim, five-foot-nine at best, and could eat more than anyone I knew. It was unusual that he would forget about lunch, but a lot did happen since this morning.

"Do you have any suggestions on what we should use for money?" Andy asked.

"I just might have an idea. Do you have any dimes or quarters?"

"Sure, but what good are they going to do us here?"

"Give me your change, then follow me and find out," I said. I had an idea all right, but my confidence in its success was a little shaky. Still, I enjoyed the fact that I thought of something that Andy didn't. He looked puzzled but didn't say anything as we walked along heading toward downtown. I was looking for the U. S. Trust bank that was across from the church. I certainly didn't expect it to have the same name, and the church wasn't there, but I was happy to discover that a bank was in the same vicinity. The new name was the Massachusetts Provincial Bank.

"Stand out here; I'll be back soon," I said, moving toward the entrance.

"You're not going to rob the place, are you?" Andy asked. I assumed he wasn't serious.

"I hope not," I answered and opened the door.

On the inside, the bank didn't look anything like I remembered. This bank had an old polished wood counter instead of the modern synthetic look, and there were no computer screens. The bank offices faced the street that I walked in from. I didn't want to go to a teller, so I walked over to the manager's office. He was in, but he was busy with a well-dressed lady customer. Well, some folks still had money, I thought, as I prepared to wait. After a few minutes of sitting around, I realized that we had seen very few men in town. There were some boys our age in the library, but that was about it. In fact, the bank manager was the first adult male I had seen since we arrived. I wondered if Andy had noticed that as well. As the woman got up to leave, the manager stood and walked her to the door. He shook her hand and waved me in. As he moved back behind his desk, I noticed that he limped as he walked, and I wondered if he had been wounded in the war.

"Well, have a seat," he said cheerfully. "What can I do for you?"

I had plenty of time to plan my approach, so I was ready. "I'm new around here, and I'm looking for a place to sell some silver. Do you buy silver at this bank?" I asked, as I took a new quarter out of my pocket and held it up in front of my face between my thumb and index finger. I positioned it so that the face of George Washington was facing him.

"Where did you get that?" he asked as he reached for it. There was no mistaking the sound of greed in his voice. I pulled it back before he snagged it, and he sat back in his chair.

"You know I could have you arrested for possession of precious metal. Bad for the war effort and very unpatriotic," he said. This was exactly the reaction that I was hoping for! I made an educated guess that a nation that had been at war as long as this might be running out of things. It appeared that my assumption was valid. And it was reasonable to assume that this society would value silver and gold the same as we did. I also took a gamble that the banker's avarice would overcome his patriotism. It may not be altruistic, but greed was universal. I wanted Andy to wait outside in case I was wrong, and this whole thing blew up. I didn't intend to risk both of us going to jail.

"I know, but I have more, and I'm guessing that you and I can make a better arrangement." He nodded and I continued, "I need a few bucks...er...pounds for a special project I'm working on. I'll sell my silver for the right price."

"What's your project?" he asked.

"I can't tell you that," I said and then added, "Besides, you don't want to know." I knew I was running the risk of spooking him, but I couldn't resist. I was getting the feeling that this guy was a real slime ball. I even began to suspect that his leg injury had a suspicious origin.

"Extra gas rations, bribery to avoid the draft, something along those lines?" He was reaching. The devil in me decided to be honest with him.

"Actually, I'm planning on using a time machine to go back in time and fix it so that this war ends."

"Very funny. How much did you have in mind?" he asked.

"Make an offer for that one," I said as I flipped him the quarter. He looked it over and quickly noticed the layer of copper between the silver sides.

"Hey, this thing isn't all silver."

"You're right; the center is copper. That's why I let you see it. I wanted you to know what you're bidding on."

"Copper, eh?" He pulled out a key chain with a magnet and tested the coin. "It's not steel, anyway. How many have you got?"

"Five," I told him. His face said it all! He probably hadn't seen this much silver in his life. I was sure he wasn't going to let this opportunity pass.

"Who else knows about this?" he asked.

"Another banker I know. She offered a pretty good price, but I figured I get a second opinion." I gambled again with the "she." I figured that in this world, there couldn't be too many male bankers with gimpy legs.

"Lee–I'll bet. She's a real piece of work." He was fishing again; I knew, but I decided to play along. I gave a slight nod, and he ran with it. "Okay, twenty pounds for the lot."

I didn't know what twenty pounds could buy in this world, but I figured this guy would start low. "Sorry I wasted your time," I said as I got up to leave.

"Okay, hold it, hold it. I meant twenty pounds each."

I still didn't know if that was worth much, but it was apparent that he thought it was. "Well, that's a little better," I told him. "But I was figuring on twice that."

"Forty pounds each, that's two hundred pounds for the lot. You think I'm crazy?" He was getting agitated now.

"My other buyer must be crazy, too," I said.

"Lee. Well if she wants them that badly, let her have 'em. I wouldn't trust her, though. She'd buy your coins *and* turn you in. My final offer is 150 pounds. That's it. Take it or leave it." His face was all red, and I decided that I didn't need to push him any harder. After all, we only needed groceries for a few days, and Andy was still waiting outside.

"Deal," I said. We made the exchange, and as I got up to leave, I asked, "How did you hurt your leg?"

"You don't want to go there. What are these things, anyway?"

"Let's just say, that is what money would look like if we had lost the American Colonial Rebellion."

"You're a funny kid. Get out already," he scowled back as I left the bank.

Andy was pacing around outside. I walked past him and told him to follow behind me until we were out of sight of the bank. We continued down what used to be Washington Street toward South Braintree Square. I took a quick glance back at the bank. The banker was watching me through his window. He dropped the curtain when he saw me turn around. I stopped just past a store front that I remembered as Richmond Hardware and waited for Andy to catch up.

"Well, are you through with the cloak and dagger stuff?" he asked as I started laughing out loud. I just couldn't help myself. Andy looked at me like I had two heads until I showed him the money. At that point, his jaw dropped and he started looking around.

"You *did* rob the bank! I thought you were only kidding!" he exclaimed.

"Actually, I just robbed the banker. Well, that's not quite true either. We made a mutually acceptable transaction. He got five quarters, and we got all this paper money."

"How did you do that?"

"Simple, I figured that with the war on, there would be lots of shortages. It would be sensible that silver and gold would be very valuable, even the small amount that is in our coins. All I needed was to find someone willing to make a deal. What better choice than a greedy banker!"

"Brilliant!" Andy exclaimed. "It never even crossed my mind to do that."

"That's why I'm here," I said, feeling very full of myself. It had been a good scam, and I didn't tell him about the fact that holding gold and silver is illegal in this world. I figured he didn't have to know that I might have ended up arrested!

"So, let's eat!" Andy yelled and headed off. Now that's more like it!

# Chapter 9—Back To The Lab

We found a little diner around the corner from the former hardware store and each of us had the blue plate special. It was meager fare, and the bread was stale, but we didn't care. At least it was filling. I didn't expect to see a diner, since that was a purely American invention, but I was pleased nevertheless. Total cost of both meals, including tip, was ten pounds. Now we knew we had enough money to last several days at least. We stopped off at a grocery store on our way back to the lab and stocked up on the essentials: cereal, bread, crackers, and some cans of soup, etc. We noticed that there was no milk at all, and other things, like butter and cheese, required ration coupons as well as money. We were happy with what we got, and we still had plenty of money left. It was early evening when we returned to the lab, but the sun was still fairly bright.

"We have time, so let's get a plan together," I said. At times like this, I was better suited to lead the effort to develop a practical plan. Andy was better at finding solutions to the technical issues that were bound to arise.

"Okay, any suggestions?" Andy asked.

"Let's start with what we expect to happen," I offered. "Our best assumption is that someone used the time machine to affect the outcome of the Battle of Trenton."

"Right, *and* we know that whoever it was will come back in approximately fifteen hours," Andy added.

"We have to make sure that we are here, in the lab, when that happens, and that all the equipment is up and running," I said.

"Check," Andy agreed. "I'll do that part. Then we can ask whomever it is what happened." Andy sometimes oversimplifies things.

"That may not be so easy. We have to plan for the worst. The person may come back dead. Killed in the battle, or he may be alive but not know what he did to change history," I said. Both of us knew that this was possible, but we hadn't talked about it until now.

"At least if he's alive, even if he doesn't know what happened, we can figure it out by asking the right questions," Andy said.

"Once we find out what happened, how do we fix it? Can you send me back in time to stop whomever it was from doing whatever he did?" I asked, knowing that what I said sounded confusing.

Andy shook his head. "I can't offer any guarantees about that. We only have two tests. In each one, the time machine moved a person through space and landed them at a time when a significant event occurred–you at Gettysburg in 1863, and our unknown traveler at Trenton in 1776. For all we know, something else has happened at Trenton since then, and the machine may send you there this time." Andy was somber, but it was the truth. We could only be sure that the time machine would send me to Trenton, not that I would arrive in the correct time period. I couldn't see any way around that problem and neither could Andy.

"We have to try, though," I said.

"Yes. We have to try," Andy agreed. "Anyway, I'll make sure the time machine is working properly. I have a few things to check out and it's going to take some time. You might as well relax. This is turning into one heck of an adventure. Someday, *I'd* like to go on one of these trips."

I wondered when he was going to get around to that. "You'll get your turn, but you know we both need you here working the controls this time. That's what you get for being a genius, Einstein." That cheered him up a little, and he started looking over the equipment. I knew what I wanted to do, but I figured that I'd better check with the master first.

"If you don't need me, I think I'll take a little stroll," I said.

"Good idea. You'll just be bored here. Oh, and say 'Hi' to Amy for me."

I hated being that transparent to Andy, but when you've been friends with someone for this long, it happens. "I will," I said and headed for the South Shore Plaza.

# Chapter 10–The Nightmare Continues!

The road to the plaza was very different from what I remembered. In my world, it was two lanes on each side when you approached the entrance on Granite Street. Here, the road was still called Granite Street, but it was one lane each way. It was evening now, but still there were few cars on the road. The movie theater was gone, and the ponds on the edge of the plaza, long filled in my world, were still in place here. Also, the plaza was small and open–as a true plaza would be–and had few stores. This place was tiny compared to my South Shore Plaza and seemed more a gathering place than a shopping center, although, from what we saw at the market, I shouldn't have been too surprised. Most products were probably going toward the war effort. If Amy and her friends were still here, they wouldn't be hard to find.

People sort of milled around, passed pleasantries, and nodded a lot. Like I noticed downtown, there were no men other than retirees and teenagers. I looked in the windows of a few stores. Mostly clothes, shoes, and basics like cloth and food. There were very few frivolous items or things associated with leisure time. After I had spent about a half an hour wandering around, I spotted a store called the Disc Shop next to the orange roof of a Howard Johnson restaurant. The name of the shop surprised me. I figured that this world hadn't experienced the computer revolution yet. I went in expecting to find electronic equipment, games, and CDs, but in fact, the store sold *vinyl records*. At least that was consistent with what we had seen so far, and it was there that I ran into Amy and her friends.

"Hi Mark, I didn't think you were coming," she said. I enjoyed hearing her voice again.

"Andy and I had to do more work on our history project," I answered.

"Did your friend come, too?" she asked, looking around.

"No, he went home to work on it some more." I sounded lame, even to myself.

"I'm glad *you* came anyway. I never introduced you to my friends," she said and proceeded to rattle off five names that I wouldn't begin to remember. I nodded politely and said that I was pleased to meet them. I was happy to notice that they began to quietly move away from us when Amy and I resumed our conversation.

"Are you looking for anything in particular?" I asked. "Maybe I can help you find it."

"Not really. I like that new song by John Lennon, *Give Peace a Chance.* I think his music is great even though he's really old." I'd heard of John Lennon. He was one of the Beatles, and my dad has all their CDs. In my world, Lennon was murdered in New York City before I was born, but he'd already made that song so I was familiar with it. It was one of Dad's favorites.

"I like that one, too. Of course I like the sentiment even more. Come on, I'll buy you an ice cream," I said as I took her hand and led her out of the store.

"Ice cream? There hasn't been ice cream in town since the war began," Amy said. "My grandfather told me about it once, but I've never had any. Where do you come from?"

I should have thought of that. Dairy products would be too precious to waste on taste treats. "Well, what do they have in that restaurant?" I asked, pointing to the restaurant and ducking her question altogether.

"Pie, and maybe some sandwiches."

"Okay, let's have some pie then."

The little shop wasn't very crowded, and we sat down at a booth near the back. The menu was unimaginative. The pie varieties were limited to rhubarb, strawberry, and strawberry rhubarb. For sandwiches they had peanut butter and jelly. The waitress came over and took our order. We both decided on the strawberry pie. Clearly, this society didn't have the material things that I was used to, but Amy and her friends seemed happy. Were they really happy or just keeping a very British stiff upper lip? I decided to find out.

"I'm from up north, so this is all a little new me. What's it like living in Braintree?" I began.

"It's okay, I guess. Not much to do. You're looking at the hot spot in town," she said. "Pretty sad, huh?"

I decided to lie. "Not at all! At least you have a place where people can come and get together. My town is small, and the people live farther apart. School is about the only place that we have to meet other people. Now *that* is sad."

"You're right," she said as she smiled. "I guess I can't complain."

This was becoming awkward so I decided to jump right into it. "Have you ever thought about how it would be without the war? I mean, not to have our whole society working to destroy an enemy most of us will never see?"

"I didn't before. I mean, when I was younger, I thought how lucky the boys were to be able to grow up and fight the Germans, or travel all the way to Australia to fight the Japanese. You know how they teach you in school–that the British Empire is great and must defeat her evil enemies before they conquer the world. I accepted it because everyone else did. But now, it seems like such a waste. Before he died, my grandfather told me stories about what it was like before the war. How people had so much, and everyone was happy. The newspapers didn't have death pages and war accounts. He said that everyone has it harder now."

I hadn't expected that! I was used to my grandfather telling us about how easy we have it, and I know that he's right. This society looks back with cheery nostalgia to the 1930s! The people here are far from oblivious to the destruction brought on by the war. Instead, they've grown accustomed to it; they've even adapted to the routine! I guess it's just human nature to try to make the best of a bad situation, but somehow this didn't seem like living at all. She was looking sad now, but I didn't want her to stop talking. I was learning so much, and it seemed to ease some of her pain to talk to someone. "I take it that you don't envy the boys anymore," I said.

"I guess that's true. As I grew up and paid more attention, I began to realize how few men returned for good. And those who did were permanently hurt in some way. Arms and legs missing, eyes shot out. That's what finally woke me up. You must have seen it up north, too."

"I have, but I always hope to be the one that makes it back." I was lying of course. I could barely imagine living in a world like this, but I felt as though I had to say something.

"Do your grandparents tell you what it was like before the war?"

"Not much, my dad says…"

*"Your dad's still alive?"* Amy asked as though she just heard some incredible revelation. Then just as quickly she added softly, "Oh, I'm sorry. Was he badly hurt?"

I knew that I had to think of something quick after that. "He lost part of his left leg–from the knee down–but I hardly even notice it."

"That must be great. Having your dad at home. You're the only one I know that has a full family. My grandfather told me it used to be like that, but I never saw it! My dad was killed just after I was born. My older brother is in the army now. He and his wife have two kids and next year, when the youngest turns six and starts school, my sister-in-law will go to work in a munitions factory. You know how it is. Most of my friends–the ones that you met–are sixteen now, so they'll be married next year. Soon after that they'll start having babies. The boys go into the training camps when they turn eighteen. They come home on leave frequently over the next three years then it's overseas by the time they're twenty-one. Most are killed before they're twenty-five. The training is prolonged to give them every opportunity to father more soldiers for the war effort. A terrible waste, isn't it?"

A meek "I know" was all I could manage. This place was getting uglier by the minute! Young people had no hope here! Their whole future was preordained. The boys went to war, and the girls stayed home, took care of the children, and worked to manufacture war materiel. I could only imagine what the Germans and Japanese were doing. Both societies were models of efficiency. Making soldiers would be considered just another productivity challenge. I imagined huge breeding camps where babies were born, and boys began military training when they could walk. British North America would be a paradise compared to Europe and Asia. I also had the feeling that the British were being forced to match the Axis techniques to keep up. They hadn't reached the level of breeding camps yet, but it was only a matter of time. Of course, the atomic bomb would change all that. Absentmindedly, I took out a dime that I still had in my pocket and began to spin it on the table.

"Do you live with your mom?" I asked.

"No. My mom was killed in a munitions factory explosion ten years ago. My grandparents never got over the shock and passed away soon after. I've been living in the Children's Home since."

"I'm sorry. I didn't know." My heart was breaking and I took her hand. She looked up at me and smiled. "It's okay. The Children's Home isn't too bad. The caretakers can be mean sometimes, but I've learned to live with it. They call it a Children's Home because orphanage sounds too harsh. Funny isn't it. I think Children's Home sounds harsh, too." I agreed because I didn't know what else to do. She told me this joyless story without a hint of sorrow. It was as if she accepted her fate and was determined not to let it beat her.

"How about you? Will you be married next year?" I asked.

"I don't even have a boyfriend, but that won't matter. I know that out in the country it's different, but here, when my time comes, someone will be picked for me. I might even have to share a husband with another girl if none are available. I'm not looking forward to that." The sadness had returned to her voice.

"It's not much different out in the country," I began. "If I don't meet a suitable girl, I'll be matched up with someone from another small town. I'll likely have to marry someone I've never met, maybe a lady whose previous husband was killed." I was making it up as I went along, but it seemed in character with this place.

"How sad," she answered as she patted my face. For all she knew, I had a family and a home. She lived alone in an orphanage, and she still felt compassion for me! Amy may be a sixteen-year-old girl, but she is quite possibly the strongest person I've ever met.

We had finished our pies, and I was surprised to see that the waitress was obviously getting ready to close the shop. I looked at my watch and saw that it was only 8:00 p.m. The dime that I was spinning earlier fell on the floor by Amy's chair. She picked it up, looked it over, and returned it. If she noticed anything strange, she didn't tell me. I quickly put it away, thinking about how stupid I was to bring it out in the first place.

"Well, I guess we should be going," Amy said.

"It's early yet, would you like to go somewhere else?" I asked. I truly enjoyed her company, but our conversational subject matter was very depressing, and I didn't want to leave her on that note.

"Oh, that's right! You don't have curfew up north. Here we have to be off the streets by dark for the black out. The streetlights stay off, and only military police and emergency vehicles are allowed on the road. I hope you'll be a gentleman and walk me home, though."

"Of course, mademoiselle, it would be my distinct pleasure," I said in my best French accent as I kissed her hand. I did British better than French, but Amy didn't seem to mind.

"Oh, how gallant." She played right along.

We walked up Granite Street toward Five Corners. As it turned out, Amy lived on Central Avenue, which wasn't far from where our houses used to be. It took a full forty-five minutes to cover the distance. To turn the subject to more cheerful matters, I asked her what she thought the world would look like now if the war had ended fifty years ago. We turned it into a game with Amy describing happy families and the end of poverty, and me pretty much describing how my world really was. I hadn't thought much about it before. Television and the newspaper articles always seem to describe the worst parts of the human condition, and I know that my world is far from perfect, but what I'm sure of now is that the developed nations in my timeline have a lot for which to be thankful.

# Chapter 11—Trading Worlds

I kissed Amy good night at her house and headed back to the lab. We had made plans to meet in the morning back at the library. It was dark now, so I made sure to cut through backyards and hide in the shadows when the patrols passed. They were easy to avoid, and I figured that not much happened around here that required their attention. When I got to the lab, Andy was drinking some canned fluid and flashing his light at a wire connection between the generator and the sending platform. He was concentrating hard on what he was doing and didn't see me come in. I couldn't resist having a little fun. I was still pumped from being with Amy all evening. I sneaked up near him and in a loud voice let him have it. "HEY ANDY, HOW'S IT GOING?"

Andy gets this great scared face when he's startled, and he didn't disappoint me this time. He jumped three feet and started to yell, *"Mark! Why do you do that! Some day you're going to give me a heart attack. Good thing it wasn't today or you'd be stuck here!"* Andy usually got mad after I startled him like that. I was laughing so hard that tears were rolling down my face. He saw me doubled over and started to recover.

"I really wish you wouldn't do that. My nerves are all twitchy now," Andy said.

I was still laughing when I apologized. "I'm sorry, bud. I just couldn't resist."

"Sure. You sound real sorry. You must have had a good evening with Amy. What did you find out?"

I told him everything. Well almost everything, I figured he didn't need to know that I kissed her good night. I explained the curfew, the social expectations of marriage by seventeen, babies by eighteen and for boys, training and battle by twenty-one. He had a predictable reaction–shock. Especially when I told him how most men never make it past twenty-five, and that those who do come home are maimed in some way.

"This place is worse than a *nightmare!*" he said, after I finished with everything. "It seems crazy to go to school, learn everything, and get killed before you use any of the knowledge."

"They still need to learn how to read, write, and do some math to be useful to the army. Also, history and social studies are ideal for whipping up the patriotic spirit."

"I guess you're right," Andy replied. "I was wrestling with my conscience a little about whether we should interfere, but I don't have any such delusions now!"

"I *never* had any qualms about returning the timeline to its proper sequence. Just think about what's probably happening in Europe right now! All the Jews have no doubt been exterminated, along with any Poles, Czechs, and Slavs that aren't in slave labor camps. And the Nazis may be about to get the atomic bomb! You said yourself that that alone was enough incentive to reverse this *madness*!" I hadn't realized it, but I was shouting now. I stopped and looked around, sincerely hoping that no one had heard me. Andy came over and patted me on the shoulder.

"Most of the people that are here now will probably no longer exist as soon as the timeline is restored. You understand that your friend, Amy, will be one of them," Andy said quietly. "Are you okay with that?"

Andy brought up something that I hadn't thought of before. Most of these people will simply go away, at least those that were affected by the disruption in time. And from what I could tell, that was everyone that I saw so far. It's not as though I was moving away and would never see them, or her, again–I was always prepared for that–but to think that she, and everyone else, would be wiped clean from the face of the Earth was hard to take. Their lives, as pointless as they seemed to us, were still lives.

"We could take her with us. We could bring her in here when the timeline is restored, and she'll become part of our world." I was beginning to sound desperate.

"Taking her with us is a tough call. Where do we draw the line? Do we try to cram as many people as possible into here? If we do that, we won't be able to keep the time machine a secret any longer. Remember what Dad said. The technology would almost certainly be misused. We can't take that risk."

Andy was right, of course. I didn't like the idea, but we couldn't pass judgement on some *or one* individual without considering the whole. Also, Andy's dad knew that if word got out that a time machine had been invented, the temptation to use it would be too great. Heck, up until now no one knew about it but Andy, his parents, and me, and we had already had a major accident.

"Okay, I understand. I just freaked out for a minute. The impact of that was a little overwhelming," I said.

"That's what I was talking about. Nothing about time travel is easy. One event impacts every other until the end of time. In this case, we think someone who got access to our machine changed the timeline that resulted in this world. Millions died that shouldn't have. We are responsible for that, and we have to try and fix it. Even though it means that everyone here will simply go away. We're on the same page with this, right?"

I was coming to grips with the whole thing now. Because of the horror of this world, I felt more pressure than ever to stop this from happening. I would miss Amy, but I rationalized it by thinking that if she knew what had happened, she would accept it. I could never be sure of that, and I could never tell her. I decided that the best way to get my mind off everything was to stick with the plan.

"We're doing the right thing. How did you make out with your technical review?" I asked, hoping that a new focus would pull it all back together.

"Good, actually. The machine is ready to go. I calculated that our time traveling intruder should be coming back in a little over thirteen hours. Then we take it from there. There's one more thing to decide," Andy said and looked at me.

"What's that?"

"I can adjust the recall time to anything that we want. How much time do you think it will take to resolve this problem? I mean, should I set the recall time to fifteen minutes, or twenty-four hours, or something in between?" Andy returned.

I was a little puzzled. "You're asking *me* that?"

"Well, you're the experienced one here," he replied. "You should get the first call. Remember that you have to find the guy and stop him. Keep in mind that you may have to use force. A longer time makes the location part easier, but if you find him quickly, you'll have to keep him quiet longer. And that may not be so easy."

"I see your point. If I use a shorter time, I run the risk of not finding him at all," I added. "But we could just try again, right?"

"Theoretically, we could try again, but we have only enough fuel in the generator to return our intruder and send you on one round trip. Also, the connections on the mains here," Andy motioned to the wires he was examining when I first startled him, "are not going to hold much longer. I'm sure that I can't get new components in this world."

"Ouch, I wish you hadn't told me that part." I was sincere about that. The last thing I needed was one more thing to worry about.

"I had to. You should know about the...*what was that*?"

"I don't know, but I heard it, too. Let's go." Someone or something was rustling the leaves outside. Either a patrol had found us, or some large animal had come by. Both of us were running to the side door. I got there first and stopped Andy from running out into the woods. We both looked around, but we didn't see anything. I motioned for Andy to move over on the right, and I would take the left side of barn.

"Meet back here in two minutes," I said. Andy nodded and we moved out. The brush was thick underfoot, and there was no moon to see by. I tried being quiet, but my motion through the foliage was creating a racket. If it was a patrol, it was gone by now. I doubted that any of the militia would come in here anyway. I worked my way around to the front of the barn and still saw nothing. I doubled back and met Andy at the door to the lab.

"See anything?" I asked.

"Nothing at all. Maybe it was a dog or something," Andy replied. That was probably it. We stood quietly listening at the door, but other than the occasional sounds generated by the wind, we heard nothing. After about five minutes we went back inside.

"I don't know about you, but I'm ready for a snack," Andy said as he walked over to the stockpile we bought earlier.

"Best idea I've heard all day," I added as I grabbed some canned ham to go with a can of fluid. I didn't know what this stuff was, but at least it was wet. As we munched out, I had to ask one more question.

"Andy, what if we're wrong? What if the call back routine is activated and no one comes back? We don't have a plan for that."

"I know. If that happens, we'll never know the details of how the Hessians were alerted and what it is that we need to fix. I still can't see how this could have happened any other way. I mean someone *had* to have gone back and done this, right?"

Oh, oh. Andy was asking me, now. I didn't expect him to have doubts about this, but I agreed with him. It seemed the most logical explanation. "I guess you're right; all we can do is wait."

"That's it," Andy said.

We planned our activities for the next day. Andy figured that the time traveler would be brought back around noon. Fortunately, he was able to find a working transmitter, and he wanted to spend the morning setting frequencies and making sure that everything worked. I found a notebook and decided to write down what I had discovered today. It wasn't very often that you actually find answers to questions like: What would have happened if the British won the Revolution? I was determined to record as much as possible before I had a chance to forget.

The cellar floor was cold and hard, but it was all we had. We found some rags and rolled them up to put under our heads for pillows. We talked well into the night about what we had seen so far. Before I fell asleep, I thought of what had happened to us during the course of the day. It started out innocently enough with a morning game of baseball on our usual field at Thayer Academy. As we left the park, neither Andy nor I could have predicted that some individual would change everything that we–or the rest of the world–knew in the blink of an eye! It had happened, and I half expected that when I woke up the next morning, it would have all been a bad dream. I tried not to think that if we were a little slower, we would have disappeared like everyone else in our world. That would have made it impossible to correct the mistake. One thing was certain. We had found the answer to the question of whether it was possible to change history with the time machine. The answer was an emphatic *Yes!* But would we be successful in changing it back? Would I be transported back to Trenton during a time when it was possible to stop what happened? Would I know what to do when I got there? There were too many questions rolling through my head. Eventually, I calmed down and dropped off to sleep. My last thoughts were of Amy standing at the door to the Children's Home as I turned to walk back to the lab.

# Chapter 12—Preparation For The Mission

Andy was already fiddling with the transmitter when I woke up. It was about 8:00 a.m., so I had about four hours until the time traveler returned. I was getting a little tense about the mission. I decided to start calling it that since that word seemed to better describe what we were trying to do now that "the plan" had been thought out.

"Well, sleeping beauty, you've decided to wake up," Andy said. "You slept all right, I see."

"I did," I answered. "How about you?"

"Well, you snored a lot, but my mind was racing too fast to sleep much anyway. After today, I plan on crashing. How about breakfast?"

"Sounds good to me!" I realized that I was very hungry. I could have used a shower too, but that wasn't going to happen. Andy and I opened up a box of cereal and started shoving the contents down our throats. It was kind of fun eating like savages without our mothers around to slap us for behaving like pigs. I wished that we had some milk, though. We made the best of it and washed down the cereal with more warm, canned whatever. For future reference, I don't recommend it. We had beef jerky for dessert. That was pretty good.

I told Andy that I was going back to the library to see Amy one last time. I could tell that he was a little uncomfortable with that, but he didn't say much. I also figured that I'd read up on the Battle of Trenton. I was going to take any edge that I could get. I was especially looking for weather conditions and actions as they related to the time of day. Also, I needed to know as much as possible about the layout of the battlefield and the surrounding area. If I could figure out how much area I had to cover, I'd have a better idea about how long the search would take. That would affect our decision on what to set the call back time to. "I'm going now," I called to Andy. "I'll be sure to be back before our friend arrives."

"Okay. I know that you're seeing Amy, but remember that you have a lot to catch up on before you go." Andy was sounding like my mother, but I knew that he was just worried.

"I know. Don't worry, I won't do anything that will jeopardize the mission."

"The mission, huh? I like that." And for the first time today, I saw Andy smile. "You look pretty grubby. Are you sure you want her to see you like that?"

"No choice. I'll think up some excuse," I said. I hadn't thought of that before, but there really was no way around it. I retraced the steps that Andy and I made the day before. It was hard to believe that it had been less than twenty-four hours since our adventure began. I looked at everything a little differently this time. What I saw made more sense now. The yards of the houses were messy. This was not surprising since a society using up significant resources on a war would hardly give a high priority to landscaping, and besides, working mothers wouldn't have the time.

I looked at my watch when I reached the library–9:00 a.m. The walk had taken about twenty minutes. I made a mental note to make sure I left the library no later than 11:30. That would give me ten minutes leeway in case something came up, or the time traveler arrived early. The latter wasn't a likely scenario since the machine operated on a timer. Amy wasn't anywhere to be seen, so I went directly to the history section.

Finding material wasn't any problem. This battle was well documented once it started, but the events leading up to the actual clash of arms were a little sketchy. Unfortunately, the details of those events were what I needed most. General Washington planned a surprise attack just before dawn on December 26, 1776. He began to move the Continental army across the

Delaware River the night before, but he was delayed by the weather. Conditions had turned nasty during the crossing. A winter storm, with sleet and freezing rain, had blown in. It was good for providing cover, but it slowed everything down. A Hessian outpost on the road to Trenton discovered the movement and alerted the main army. The army commander decided to allow Washington to think that his surprise was working, and he kept his men ready but out of sight in a semicircle covering the roads leading into town. He used the town itself as bait to lure the Continental army in so that the Hessians could surround and destroy it.

When the Continentals reached Trenton, the Hessians sprung the trap and captured, or killed, the entire main body of the army. Washington managed to escape the initial snare, but he was captured a short time later trying to re-cross the Delaware to the original camp. The history book that I was reading made a big deal about Washington's disgrace at abandoning his men and fleeing to save his own neck. It was hard to read about our first president being described as a cowardly figure, and it was making me sick all over again, but like Andy said, the winners write the history books.

I browsed the shelf and found a small but well detailed book with the simple title *The American Colonial Rebellion.* It contained more information about the decisive battle at Trenton, and I decided that I would "borrow" the book even though I didn't have a library card. I rationalized the theft by figuring that if Andy and I were successful, the book would be an interesting reminder of our adventure, and no one would be the wiser. Andy could use it as a reference and give me details, as I needed them, after the mission was underway. It also had a map of the area as it looked at the time of the battle.

A glance at my watch indicated the time to be 11:00 a.m., and Amy was still not in sight. I opened the book and decided to read for the next thirty minutes. As I started, Amy arrived. I was glad to see her and smiled immediately. She smiled back, but I couldn't help noticing that it seemed a little forced. Her eyes didn't light up the way they did last evening, and she looked stiff when I tried to kiss her. Maybe she was tired.

"I'm glad you made it. I was about to give up," I started. "Is everything all right?"

"I had some things I had to do at the Home," Amy replied. "What are you reading?" I showed her the book, and she continued. "You and your friend are really serious about this project, aren't you?"

"Let's just say that our whole little world sort of depends on it."

We chitchatted a little more about last evening until it was time for me to go. I would have liked to take her with me. It was hard not to tell Amy our story, and somehow I felt as though I was betraying her, but that couldn't be helped. We made plans to meet again that evening at the plaza. I didn't see anything wrong with spending another evening with Amy if the mission had to be postponed for a while. We said our good-byes and I headed back to the lab. When I reached the sidewalk, I turned around to wave and saw the greedy banker standing on the other side of the street about a block away. I didn't know why he was there, but it didn't seem likely that he was waiting for a bus. When he saw that I recognized him, he turned away and started to walk off toward the bank. I waved at Amy again and didn't give the banker another thought.

I had one more duty to perform before reaching the lab. I stopped off at a clothing shop that I saw earlier and purchased a heavy coat and some long pants. I had to ask for the items since the racks were filled with summer wear. I held my breath until the clerk came back with a few selections. The coat was woolen with a nylon liner. The pants were made of brown cotton. Neither made a fashion statement, but they would serve my purposes well enough. I was anticipating that Trenton, New Jersey, on Christmas, 1776, would be very cold indeed.

I ran back to the lab to make up some of the time that I lost in the clothing store, and I arrived a few minutes early. Andy was eating again and looking at the computer screen. He heard me this time but didn't look up.

"I've been looking at the program," he said excitedly. "Once the timer counts down, it simply moves to the next line which calls the return subroutine. I inserted a line that stops the program until the operator presses this button. See?" Andy waved me over to the screen. On the computer screen he had placed a button labeled "Call Back."

"Point and click, and the program continues, and the return subroutine is activated," he said, clearly delighted with himself.

I couldn't quite see the point in it so I asked, "What good is that? Wouldn't it be better to let the program run automatically?"

"Well, this way we can set the call back timer to something short–say five minutes–and then use the button to bring the time traveler back based on our communications. A quick exit, so to speak, if necessary."

*Now* I saw the advantage, but I had one more question. "That sounds good, but what if our communications fail and you don't hear from me?"

"We revise our own procedure to include a previously agreed maximum time," Andy began. "Say we decide that the mission will take a maximum of twelve hours. We can still set up the timer to call back in five minutes. After that goes by, I can call you back whenever you say. Now if we lose contact, I'll stick to the original plan and push the button after twelve hours."

"Not a bad idea," I said.

"We'll get to try it soon, the timer is winding down. The code to call back the time traveler will move to execute the next line, which now is the one that I inserted. I'll have to push the button before the call back subroutine is executed. If it doesn't work, I'll simply remove the line."

At that moment, the lab suddenly grew dark. Both Andy and I looked up. The bodies of several people were blocking the outdoor light. My eyes hadn't adjusted to the darkness yet, but I couldn't mistake the distinct outline of the greedy banker standing out in front!

# Chapter 13–The Spy

The banker moved into the cellar. He was the tallest of the group, and by the way the others looked at him, it was clear that he was the leader. He gave the room a once over that took in all the computer equipment, the transporter platforms, and the massive antennae by the computer work-station. Since the generator was outside, and not far from the door, I was sure that he saw that, too. He didn't say much, but you could see his mind making mental notes when his eye caught something of interest. And I could tell by watching the points at which his gaze stopped, that he knew the important items to study. I thought to myself while I watched all this, that I had badly misjudged the man. He no longer resembled the greedy lowlife waiting for opportunity. He was commanding and appeared fear-less. Exactly what he was in command *of* was still a mystery. As my eyes completed their adjustment, I saw that the group consisted of boys and girls around my age with a few old men mixed in–about a dozen in total. A shorter figure moved from the back of the pack to stand next to the tall man. My heart sank to see that it was Amy!

The banker spoke first, "Do you mind telling me what all this equip-ment is and how it got here?"

Andy was still standing at the computer terminal but it was he who answered, "Who wants to know?"

"Ask your friend," he said, motioning to me. "Surely he's told you about me."

Andy looked at me as I said, "He's the banker from downtown that I sold the quarters to," then more loudly, "apparently he wasn't satisfied with that."

"It's not like that, Mark," Amy answered. "The coins that you sold are stamped, 'The United States of America.' The same was on the coin you dropped on the floor in the pie shop. That term is usually associated with the dissident movement."

Being referred to as a dissident caught me by surprise. Was it possible that the American Rebels maintained an underground network that was waiting for another opportunity to rise up? After over two hundred years, I highly doubted it, but what else could these coins be interpreted as? Still, seeing Amy with this group was unnerving, and I had to know more.

"Amy, how did you find us?" I asked.

"I followed you after you walked me home," she answered. "I had to."

"It was you we heard last night. Wasn't it?" Andy asked.

Amy didn't try to hide it. "Yes. I hid in the woods until you stopped looking."

"But *why*?" I asked. "We are *not* dissidents, and who are these people with you?"

"I'm afraid we can't tell you that," the banker said. "At least not until we learn a little more about you. It could be that our causes are more related that you think." He hadn't bought the denial.

Andy spoke next, "Mark is right; we aren't dissidents, and we have no cause."

The banker's expression became stern. "Look. This setup here," he said, as he opened his arms and turned indicating the time machine equipment in the cellar, "has been brought here for some reason. Why don't you start by telling us what it is and how it got here?"

"Why should we tell you?" I asked. "We don't even know who you are."

"That makes us even. We don't know who you are either, do we? But we know that you're new in town, and based on what I see here, we could have you picked up by the military police in twenty minutes. I don't think you'd like that." Well, at least we knew that *this* crowd wasn't the MPs. That was a relief!

"I don't think you'd like our explanation," Andy said.

"*Try me*!" The banker was getting testy.

"Well, it's like this," Andy began, "this is a time machine, and the world was never meant to be this way. We come from a world where the Rebels won the American Revolution, and World War II ended in 1945! In victory, I might add, by the combined forces of the British Empire, the Soviet Union, and United States among others. The United States led the war effort!"

I couldn't believe that Andy told them all this! It was true of course, but there was no chance that this group was going to believe it!

The banker continued, "I can see that you're not going to cooperate." Then to his compatriots he said, "Take them."

"No, wait!" Amy said to him and then turned to me. "Mark, please tell us what you're doing. The military police will hurt you if they find out about any of this. I know you're not from around here. And you're not like anyone that I have ever met before. I don't expect your explanation to be simple, but please give us some reason to believe you."

I could tell by her eyes that she wanted to give us every chance to explain ourselves. I was touched, but there wasn't much that I could say. Andy had spoken the truth. Maybe my tone of voice would help. "Amy, I know that Andy's explanation sounds far-fetched. Last night, when I described what the world would look like if the war ended fifty years ago, I was telling you what our world is like."

Amy shook her head and sighed, "Oh, Mark."

"I just wish there was some way that we could prove it," I said dejectedly and hung my head. But it was too late. The banker's cronies were on us in seconds. I managed to give the first one to reach me a bloody nose, but there were too many of them. They pushed both Andy and me to the ground and held us there. I was infuriated but I was powerless to free myself.

The banker stepped forward and stood over us. "We'll get to the truth now, people." He turned around. "Doctor," the banker called to a short, rotund man. He must have been in the back of the crowd, because I didn't see him earlier. I guessed him to be middle-aged. His face was red with flabby jowls. His clothes were clean but tight. He pulled a syringe, and a vial of some drug, from a small, black leather bag. He spoke to the banker before he filled it.

"Which one?" he asked.

"Shoot the skinny one. We've been watching the big kid."

"Okay," the doctor replied. He was going to inject the drug into my friend! Andy started to struggle again, and I freaked!

"WHAT IS THAT? WHAT ARE YOU DOING?" I shouted. "LET US UP YOU NAZI QUACK!"

"SHUT HIM UP!" the banker replied. Instantly, I was gagged with what I guessed to be a belt. "This is truth serum. Harmless, but very thorough. The best our fine chemists have developed. It's used routinely to determine whether any of our own spies have turned. It has no lasting effects."

That didn't make me feel any better, but there was nothing that I could do. The doctor pushed up Andy's sleeve and gave him the shot. Andy struggled, but within a minute he was quiet and staring straight ahead. The men holding him down let him go. Andy didn't move. The doctor helped him up and guided him to the bench. The drug was powerful, all right. Andy was very compliant and seemed content to do exactly what the doctor instructed.

"What is your name?" the doctor asked, in a kind and friendly voice. He seemed to be going out of his way to be gentle. Clearly, this was no sadistic monster. Maybe there was a spark of humanity to be found here, yet.

"Andy Royce." Andy's speech was thick and slurred but he was grinning and starting to giggle. He certainly wasn't feeling any pain. I hoped they were right when they said that it was harmless.

"How old are you?"

"Sixteen."

"And where do you live, Andy?"

"Braintree, Mathachuzetzs."

The doctor and the banker exchanged surprised looks. "Are you sure it's working, Doctor," the banker asked.

"It's never failed that I know of. I'd stake my reputation that he's telling us the truth–at least the truth as he sees it. Here, I'll show you."

"Andy, I want you to tell me a secret. A secret that you wouldn't want anyone to know."

Andy laughed. "Katie, has a crush on me. But shhhh…don't tell Mark. I think she's a cute kid." Oh, oh, I guess he knew. The thought of Katie made me smile. At least I *would* have smiled if I weren't gagged.

"Very well, continue, Doctor."

"Now Andy, what street do you live on?"

"Oak Hill Road. It used to be here. Ha, ha! But not noowww." Andy was almost singing. He was clearly enjoying himself.

More glances around the room. I heard someone mutter that there was no Oak Hill Road.

"What year is this, Andy?"

"The year two thoushan' and something."

"That's the only one he's gotten right," the banker said.

"What country do you live in, Andy?"

"The United States of 'merica." This brought murmurs from the group.

"And where are you, now?"

"Braintree, Mathachusetzs."

"What country are you in now?"

"British Norf 'merica."

"How did you get here, Andy?"

"The time machine brought British Norf 'merica to here," Andy said and began to giggle. He looked at Amy. "Mark, thinks you're cute," he giggled again. Amy looked at me and blushed.

"The kid must be deluded," the banker said.

"Maybe. But he really believes this."

"Andy, can you tell us how the time machine brought British North America here?"

"I think someone…the Hessians…woke up. Suposhed to be drunk. But noooo."

"He's not making any sense. Did you give him too much?" the banker asked the doctor.

I tried to yell, "I'll translate." but all that came out was a garbled "rrrr rrrrrrr rrrrrr."

Amy spoke next, "I think Mark wants to tell us what he said."

I growled again and nodded my head. The banker came and stood over me. "Is that what you want, to tell us what the other kid said?" I nodded my head again.

"Okay, but any noise from you, and we're gagging you again. Understood?" More nodding. I certainly didn't want to be gagged a second time. The belt tasted gross.

"Undo the gag," he ordered.

I cracked my jaw and spit. "What Andy's trying to say," I began, turning to the banker, "is that after reading your history books and comparing them to the facts we remembered from our timeline, we have been working under the assumption that someone used the time machine and prevented the Rebels from winning the Battle of Trenton in 1776. That interference caused the Rebels to lose the war and the Revolution ended."

"That's crazy! Doctor, see if the kid knows why Mark, here, was buying a winter coat in August. Maybe that will explain something." I'll admit that I wasn't looking for a tail during my walks around town, but these guys didn't miss much.

The doctor turned back toward Andy. He put his hand on his shoulder in what looked like an attempt to reassure him. My friend didn't look like he needed reassurance. He looked like he needed coffee. The strong, perked kind. He was absolutely stoned! "Andy, this is important, why did Mark buy a winter coat this morning?"

"Prolly 'cuz it's cold in Trenton in winter, shilly. And it'll be snowin' don't cha kno'. Back then at the battle. It was snowin'!"

The questioning went on for another hour and covered everything from how the time machine worked to who built it and what we planned to do with it. I didn't think anyone believed anything that Andy said. They figured he was crazy–and me too, for repeating the parts they found unclear. Finally, they were near the end, when Andy dropped the bomb.

"Andy, would you be able to prove any of this?" the doctor asked.

"Shurrrr…"

"How?"

"Timer ran out by now. Push the button and the traveler comes back. Right over there." He pointed to the platform. "Simple. Even you could do it." He giggled again.

The banker went over to the screen and the keyboard. "Ask him which button?"

"Which button do you press, Andy?"

"The 'Call Back' button." Andy was hanging his head and shaking it from side to side. I heard the doctor tell the banker that there wasn't much time. Andy was coming out of it.

"Then the person who went into the past will come here?"

"Oh, I *hope* so," Andy said.

"I don't see any button labeled 'Call Back,'" the banker replied from the computer workstation.

"It's on the screen," I offered. The banker found the button and pushed the screen with his finger. I forgot that he had never seen a personal computer or a mouse before. "I could do that for you," I said.

"We don't have time for this," the banker replied. "Take them outside. We'll deal with this equipment later."

The doctor gently guided Andy to a standing position. I swore I saw my friend give me a wink as he caught my eye. Apparently he wasn't as stoned as we thought. The doctor led him along, and as he passed the computer Andy faked a stumble, reached down, grabbed the mouse, and clicked the "Call Back" button. The doctor thought he merely slipped and helped him back up. At once, I heard the generator ignite followed by the now familiar whirr of the electric field forming. Andy had started the recall sequence.

# Chapter 14—The Surprise Time Traveler

The moment of truth was here! Our new acquaintances watched in shocked silence as the time machine kicked into action. Andy and I stood still and watched as well, but I could feel the others staring at us when they weren't watching the platform. They were beginning to realize that Andy might not have been so crazy after all. Luckily for us, someone did indeed return from the past. Haze from the green glow obscured the detailed features, but whomever it was lay there, curled in a ball, shivering. At least the traveler was alive. The haze gradually faded to reveal *Andy's mom*! The sight must have given my friend an adrenaline rush. He shook off the remaining effects of the drug and rushed to the platform. With one hand, he reached down to brush his mom's hair from her eyes. Mrs. Royce is a pretty lady with long, dark hair, bright eyes, and a friendly smile, but now she was dirty, her clothes in tatters, and covered with hay. Her face was badly bruised. She'd clearly had a rough time of it. I hoped that she wasn't hurt too badly.

Andy and I never spoke about it, but if I were to hazard a guess, I would have figured the Duke to have had a hand in all this. It was he who was snooping around and asking questions. And he was the only one, outside Andy's family and I, who knew anything was even going on inside the Royces' cellar. The last thing that I expected to see was Andy's mom returning from the past. I never figured on Mrs. Royce tinkering around with the time machine. There had to be more to this!

"Mom, are you okay?" Andy asked softly. He had tears in his eyes, but he was holding it together. He looked up at me and added, "She's freezing."

I handed Andy the coat that I bought earlier, and he placed it over her. The banker was standing to my right at the edge of the platform. Amy was on my left. She slid her hand into mine as we both looked on. The banker reached down and touched Mrs. Royce's hand. "She *is* frozen!" he exclaimed. The group with him gave a collective gasp.

"It stands to reason. She just came back from December 26, 1776, in Trenton, New Jersey. These were all the clothes she had with her," I said, motioning at her with my free hand.

"We should get her outside where the sun can warm her faster," the banker said as he stepped onto the platform. "I'd recommend a hospital, but that will lead to a lot of questions none of us will want to answer. Of course, if she doesn't improve on her own, we'll have to take her anyway."

I jumped onto the platform with him, and together, the banker and I carried Mrs. Royce outside. A blast of summer heat hit us as we walked through the cellar door. It had to be over ninety in the small patch of sun shining between the shadows of the trees. On a day like this it wouldn't take Andy's mom long to warm up. As the sun beat down, Mrs. Royce began to moan softly, and I saw Andy relax as he realized that she was going to be okay. A few minutes later she opened her eyes. She recognized Andy immediately and opened her mouth to speak, but nothing came out. "Welcome back, Mom," Andy said as he rubbed her hands. "How was your trip?"

On her second attempt to speak, Andy's mom was more successful. "What happened?" It was barely a whisper.

The banker bent down to look at Mrs. Royce's face. "We were hoping *you* could tell *us*. How do you feel, ma'am."

"I'm cold, but I'm better now, thank-you. Mr.…"

"Whitman," the banker replied.

"Mom, do you remember what happened? How did you get here?" Andy asked.

"I heard something downstairs…" As she started to explain, she turned her head and saw the others gathered around. Except for me, these were people she didn't recognize. She also saw the barn and the trees and realized that her house should be there. What I saw next had to be one of the fastest recoveries from hypothermia in history. At once she sat up and looked around. She recognized the generator but little else. "Andy, *where* are we? *How* did you find me? Where's your *father*?"

"Mom, it's important that you remember exactly what happened," Andy began. "There's been an accident. We're not in Kansas anymore, but Mark and I are going to get us home."

"Isn't this our yard? And our house…it should be here!" She was beginning to get hysterical. Mr. Whitman reacted instinctively and covered her mouth with his hand. He wasn't rough, but he was firm. Amy stroked her hair and calmly whispered something to her that I couldn't hear. Andy bent down and spoke to her in a clear and concise tone.

"Mom, you've got to stay quiet. We'll explain everything soon, I promise. Do you understand?" Mrs. Royce nodded, and Whitman released her.

"I'm sorry," she said. "It's been a long day. I'm okay now."

Whitman smiled and nodded his head. "If you're feeling better now, ma'am, we should probably go back inside. It's not safe for a gathering of this size to be spotted by the patrols."

"Patrols?" Andy's mom asked.

"Yes, they can't see this place from the road very well, but if they hear anything, they may decide to investigate. You boys have some interesting equipment in there," he motioned toward the cellar door, "and I don't think we want the authorities to see it just yet."

Mrs. Royce gave Whitman a puzzled look. He caught it and commented, "You really don't understand any of this. Do you?"

"No, but I'm hoping someone fills me in on it soon," she said, giving Andy a stern look. Andy sort of raised his eyebrows and tried to look innocent. I laughed right out loud. Amy caught me and motioned me to be quiet.

Even Whitman seemed to enjoy the exchange. "Precocious youngsters can get into the most interesting mischief, don't you think, Mrs...."

"Royce. And yes, especially these two," she said, pointing an accusing finger at Andy and me.

Once inside, Andy offered his mom water and some cold canned soup as he motioned for her to sit on the bench. I was sure that fare of this kind wasn't typically on the Royces' household menu, but she ate without saying a word. I suspected that it was the first meal she'd had since her unscheduled trip into the past.

Once she'd finished, Andy tried again. "Mom, do you remember what happened. You started to say that you heard something downstairs."

"That's right. I heard some shuffling or something. I thought that you and Mark had come back from the baseball game..."

"Baseball game?" Whitman asked.

"That's actually the national sport of the United States of America. It's played with a bat and ball and...well it's too hard to explain now, but Andy and I both consider it a tragedy that it was never invented here. You're missing out on a great game," I offered in way of an explanation.

Mr. Whitman moved over to sit on the bench next to her. Looking at Andy and me, he said, "I still don't know what to make of all this, but I'm satisfied that you are not government agents. They couldn't have done this, and quite frankly, they aren't that smart. Also, there's no reason for all of us to be here." Motioning to the others of his group, he said, "The rest of you can go home. I'll fill them in on our purpose. This may be the break we've been looking for."

One member of the group started to protest. A boy, who appeared a little older than me, began to raise his voice when Whitman silenced him with a look that told us all that he considered his last statement an order. "Amy, you can stay. You and Mark may have been seen together by the patrols. We may be able to use that, too." Whitman's mysterious following left, and Andy asked his mother to continue from where she left off.

Andy's mom spoke next, "Andy, where exactly are we? This is our cellar, but everything outside looks different. After hearing Mark just now, he's speaking of the United States as though it were someplace else."

"Nothing has actually moved, Mom," Andy began. "It's just that the world around us has changed. Something happened that caused the Americans to lose the Revolution. What we knew as Canada and most of the United States is now called British North America."

"What could possibly have happened that could have caused *that*! It doesn't make any sense," Andy's mom said.

"Mark and I went to the local library to do a little research, and found that the Hessians won the Battle of Trenton. Washington was captured and the Revolution collapsed. A lot more has happened since then, but we probably don't need to get into it now."

"That damn transporter," Mrs. Royce said. "I'm having your father shut this thing down. Did you boys run another experiment without him? Honestly, Andy what did you do that caused all this?"

"I'm sorry, Mom, but it wasn't us. We haven't used the transporter without Dad since Mark's trip last month," Andy replied.

"Then who did? Who would have done such a thing?" Andy's mom was clearly angry now. I still wasn't sure that she grasped the sheer magnitude of the changes that resulted from the altered timeline.

When Andy answered, his voice was soft, "We're pretty sure that it was you, Mom. Actually, it couldn't have been anyone else. You see, when we found out what happened and activated the transporter call back sequence, all travelers that were sent during that execution of the program would have returned. You were the only one who came back. I know you didn't mean to, but something you did while you were gone caused all this."

Mrs. Royce sat in shocked silence. Andy coaxed her into continuing her story.

"I heard some noise, as I said, and I opened the cellar door to see if you and Mark wanted some lunch. Instead, I saw that Belmont boy sitting at the computer. I knew that you guys weren't friends, so I yelled down to find out what he was doing. When he heard me, he ran out, and I went down to see if anything was damaged or missing. I didn't see anything unusual, or at least more unusual than the normal stuff you and your father keep in here."

Jeff Belmont! The Duke himself! He didn't go back in time and change history, but he must have started the computer sequence that sent Andy's mom into the past! I couldn't imagine what Andy must have been thinking, but his outward expression didn't give anything away. Andy's mom continued, "I walked around a little, and when I stepped up on this platform," she indicated the sending platform, "something happened. The next thing I knew I was lying down on a dirt road in the middle of the night. The air was cold, and it was *sleeting*. I was freezing since I didn't have anything on but these." She gestured to her clothes. "I was frightened too, and with everything happening so fast, I thought I was having a bad dream."

"You were sent to Trenton," I said. "On Christmas Day, 1776."

"Well that explains the temperature and the snow. It was blowing a blizzard! All I could think of was: Where was I and how can it be snowing in August? I knew I'd freeze to death if I stayed still, so I got up and started walking down the road. It must have been nearly dawn, because I saw the distant sky lighten as I reached a farmhouse. I'm not sure though. I was so frozen by then that I was barely moving. I remember praying that someone was home when I knocked on the door. I just wanted to warm up and use the telephone. I had no idea that I was no longer in the present.

"I pounded on the door and still heard nothing from inside. I couldn't go on and I kind of collapsed and leaned on the door and fell asleep. I woke up when it opened, and I fell into the room. Everything is a little sketchy after that. I remember hearing laughter and voices, but I couldn't make it out. It sounded like gibberish. It wasn't until later, after I warmed up a little, that I realized that I was hearing German.

"I noticed that I was surrounded by four soldiers in some kind of blue uniform that I didn't recognize. I kept asking if I could use the phone, but the one that spoke English, the only one of the group that did, apparently, kept asking me where I came from and what was 'phone.' Of course, I didn't realize that none of these men had ever seen one! Eventually, the one questioning me grew frustrated and started slapping my face. I just couldn't hold up any more, and I started crying."

I saw Andy stiffen when he heard that part of the story. Mrs. Royce started crying again as she recalled the beating. Andy hugged her, and Mr. Whitman held her hand. After a few minutes she composed herself and continued, "I'm not sure how long that went on, but it was quite a while. All of a sudden, the men watching the windows became very agitated and started hooting and hollering. Three of them ran out the back door, and a few minutes later, I heard horses galloping away from the house. The last man brought me outside to a barn and locked me in. I heard him ride off as well. That's the last I knew until I came here. I crawled under what hay I could find to try and keep warm, but I was freezing, anyway."

"I suspect that you woke up a Hessian outpost," Andy said. "Once the men were awakened, they resumed their normal vigilance and spotted Washington's army. Their fast escape was probably to warn the main force at Trenton."

"Apparently, they were successful," I put in. "The book that I brought back from the library said that the Hessians were in position and waiting for Washington's men. It looks like our assumption was correct. Someone *did* go back and change history."

"Well, at least we have an explanation," Andy said.

"All that just because of me?" Andy's mom asked.

"Unfortunately, Mom, that was just the beginning," Andy replied.

# Chapter 15—Whitman's Cause

Andy brought his mom up to speed about the history of British North America. Mr. Whitman covered the gaps that we didn't know. She was just as appalled as we were that the Second World War was still going on. Amy looked stunned by the whole thing. I think she was just beginning to realize that her world was the result of a scientific project gone awry. Whitman accepted it well. He almost seemed relieved. The thought that World War II was supposed to end with an Allied victory in 1945 brought with it the realization that the death count was far higher in this world than it was in ours. We never told our visitors about the fate of the European Jews during the holocaust or the invention of the atomic bomb. We figured that we'd given them enough to swallow in one gulp.

Since we told our side of the story, I thought that it was time that Whitman leveled with us about his interest in all this. "Okay, Mr. Whitman," I began, "it's your turn. What's your group all about and why have you and your people been following me?"

"You must understand that the nature of our cause requires the utmost discretion. In short, we are an illegal organization. The government considers our actions subversive and treasonous. If we are caught, we hang. It's as simple as that. If our methods seemed harsh, I apologize, but bear in mind that the military police wouldn't have been so gentle.

"Private ownership of precious metals is illegal. You were a lucky young man that *I* was the one who saw your coins. Anyone else, and you and Andy would have been taken in by the authorities so fast you'd be dizzy. Assuming that you remained alive of course."

"Why didn't *you* call the MPs?" Andy asked.

"He already knew about you," Amy said. "I told him. After I first saw you in the library, I knew that you weren't from around here, Mark. I told you that we were going to the plaza because I wanted you to follow. I went straight to the bank when I left the library."

"I thought you liked me! That's why you told me where you were going!" I felt hurt and angry. Bait was dangled in front of me, and I was all over it like stink on dung. What a dope I was!

Amy came over, took both my hands in hers and looked me straight in the eyes. "I do like you, Mark, I really do! I was just being careful. The government uses spies all the time to try and infiltrate the movement. Most of us have lived here all our lives. New people stand out, and new people have often turned out to be spies."

"How did you know that I would be going to the bank?" I asked.

"I *didn't*! Mr. Whitman is the local head of the movement. I was only reporting what I saw. I was stunned to hear later about what you did!"

"That's why we started to watch you, Mark," Whitman said. "Tokens with 'United States of America' and eagles, and 'Independence' stamped on them have been turning up for two hundred years! *And* they're usually associated with some type of protest movement. Normally they're made of wood or plastic. Yours was the first I've ever seen made out of silver. We *had* to check you out. That's also why I bought them. If you were an agent, I simply would have told the police that I saw the silver and got greedy. I didn't realize that you held some back. When no one came to question me, I knew you weren't a spy. Also you followed Amy to the plaza."

"What's that got to do with anything?" I asked. I really didn't see any connection.

"Oh, Mark, I was so glad to see you," Amy answered. "Don't you see? A spy would have had to report his observations. It's unlikely that he'd have time to socialize. After we had pie, I knew you were okay. A little weird maybe, but all right."

"Weird?" I said indignantly.

"Okay, unusual. How's that?"

"Well, that's better," I said, as Amy gave me a bright smile and a kiss on my cheek. She certainly had a way of melting my anger. I felt that pang again when I realized that we would soon be parting forever. I didn't show it, though.

"I've heard a lot about causes and movements and tokens, but you still haven't told us who you are," Andy said. "For all we know, *you* could be government agents stalling us until the authorities get here. Either arrest us, tell us who you are, or let us get on with our mission."

"*Mission*?" Whitman and Mrs. Royce asked at the same time. Both were smiling at Andy. Everyone seems to get a kick out of hearing that for the first time.

Andy wasn't amused. "Yes? To correct history? Duh!"

Now Amy and I answered, "*Duh?*" Andy always hated that expression, and it was funny to hear him say it. It reminded him of "*not*" back in the days when *Wayne's World* was all the sensation. He was very happy when the fad finally died out. So was I, but I still used it once in a while just to hear Andy groan. I looked at Amy and asked, "All kidding aside, what is your cause?"

"Peace. It's the peace movement, Mark, and it's growing," Amy began. "It seems like the whole British Empire is represented. We have trouble organizing because of the government's watchdogs, but we'll win in the end!" She was clearly excited about the possibility. I looked at Andy and saw him shake his head ever so slightly. I gave him a wink because I knew we were thinking the same thing.

"What is your goal?" asked Andy. "A successful peace uprising here might pull the British Empire out of the war, but that'll hand the Soviet Union, and probably Africa, to the Nazis."

"The peace movement is rising in Europe, too," Whitman continued. "The plan is to stop both Nazi Europe *and* British North America from fighting. The Soviet Union will be more than happy to end their involvement in Europe and concentrate on Japan."

I didn't want to break their spirits, but I didn't have much hope that any movement other than fascism would be likely to succeed in Europe. What I remembered about the Nazis was that the fate for anyone expressing a sentiment unfavorable to the state was immediate execution. The peace movement was giving these people something to hope for, but it was a pipe dream.

"What do you know about the German super bomb?" I asked. "A peace movement in Europe would be less likely to be effective if the Nazis figured the bomb would bring them victory."

"That's true," Whitman said. "We don't have much time. That's why I'm inclined to let you continue on your mission. I'm convinced now that there's some truth to what you claim. This fine lady here," he indicated Mrs. Royce, "is sincere, and I saw with my own eyes her return in your machine. And as I said before, everything that you've done is consistent with what you've said. Mark, do you remember what you told me when I asked you what the coins were?"

"That's what money would look like if we lost the American Colonial Rebellion," I replied.

"That's right. Antagonistic, maybe, but truthful," he smiled.

It seemed like a long time since my trip to the bank. I had thought myself clever for pulling one over on the greedy banker, but now I can see that I didn't fool anyone. Actually, he was probably right. Had the authorities–or any one inclined to report me to the authorities–seen the quarters, Andy and I might well have met a most unpleasant fate. What was even more significant was that our mission would have ended, and this timeline would have remained permanent. Andy's mom would have returned half-frozen, hungry, and alone in a world that she knew nothing about. I don't know if Andy was thinking about this, but upon reflection, stumbling into Mr. Whitman was really a lucky break. Despite all that, I remembered my last question to him just before I left the bank.

"How did you hurt your leg?"

"Ah, that was a most fortunate moment." He paused to give us time to think about how a man's injury could be considered an act of good fortune. "I was shot in Egypt saving a platoon of men pinned down by Nazi machine gun fire. I still managed to crawl close enough to toss a grenade into the nest. The High Command awarded me the Victoria Cross for that. As a result, I was able to become an effective leader for the peace movement. You see, that decoration has allowed me to remain above the suspicions of the authorities, at least so far."

The Victoria Cross was the British equivalent of our Congressional Medal of Honor, and it is awarded only for acts of extreme heroism. As a recipient it seemed reasonable that he would be considered a war hero and above reproach. I found myself admiring this man for his acknowledged bravery, accomplishments, and conviction. Nevertheless, he and Amy traveled a dangerous course that likely meant a firing squad, or a hangman's noose, when they were discovered. I felt that they had earned the right to know the whole truth.

"There's one more thing that you and Amy should be aware of," I said. "If we are successful in restoring the timeline to it's original course, you and everyone you know may no longer exist."

"I have more faith than that!" he exclaimed. "I believe that we will be born, just not in this violent world. Tell me, have you seen any similarities between our Braintree and yours?"

"Well," I began, "the roads are generally laid out the same, and we did have a South Shore Plaza. And the main building of Thayer Acad…er Horatio Nelson Regional Secondary School is nearly identical to the one in our world."

"There you are," he said with a smile. "That building was built in 1869. Well after the timeline was changed. Do you really think that two separate individuals would have come up with the exact same building design?"

His argument was certainly getting my attention, but it was Andy who answered next, "No, it must have been the same man. He must have existed in both timelines."

"That's right," Whitman continued. "I prefer to believe that all of us have a counterpart in your timeline. We may not live in the same town, or even look the same, but our souls will be there."

"That's strong faith," I said.

"It is, but your own observation of the school provides some evidence. Anyway, to be exposed as members of the peace movement would mean a certain and unpleasant death. Nobody dedicated to this cause expects to grow old. For us, it's always a matter of time." He walked over to Amy and put his arm around her. "Besides, millions have died that wouldn't have if your timeline had remained unaltered. That would be reason enough to let you continue."

"But what about your families?" Andy asked.

"Neither Mr. Whitman nor I have much family left," Amy said. "And we have the war to thank for that. That's why we work so hard for the movement. The cause is just. All this killing must end so that the world can begin to live again. Any of us would gladly give our lives to stop the war. If you can do it, then we must help."

Amy looked at Whitman and I saw him smile. It was a smile of unconcealed pride. Pride in this young woman's strength and resolve. I knew that I was in the presence of the two bravest people that I would ever meet. Andy felt it, too. "Your lives here will never really end because we will remember both of you forever," he said solemnly with a tear in his eye. Andy's mom walked over and put her arms around both Mr. Whitman and Amy.

# Chapter 16–Preparation For The Journey

Andy gave the equipment the once over for what seemed liked the millionth time. Whitman and Amy helped me with the outfit that I planned to wear into the past. Amy made the excellent observation that while I might be warm in the coat that I bought earlier in the day, I would certainly look out of place in 1776. Fortunately, the coat that I had selected was long and drab. It reached down past my butt and was a sort of brownish, green color. Pounding the thing on the stones created small tears and worn spots. A dragging through the dirt infested it with an irregular coating of grime. The total effect yielded a perfectly shabby appearance. We also felt some perverse enjoyment out of messing up something that was brand new, and we repeated it with the pants. Mrs. Royce was doing the same to a blanket that she had found in the cellar. It didn't need as much work, but she went at it with gusto! In the end, we had three well-worn garments that should pass for eighteenth-century clothing–if nobody looked too closely. My plan was to wear the blanket as a kind of cape over the newer coat. With luck, it should serve well enough.

We were still missing one thing. I needed to carry another overcoat to give to Andy's mom when I caught up to her in the past. We now knew that she would be freezing by the time I found her. Amy ran home to find such a garment and when she returned, she had bad news.

"I saw Billy Hudson talking with a military police captain on the sidewalk on Central Avenue," she told us. "I think he's up to something."

"Who's Billy Hudson?" I asked.

"The boy who started the argument when I asked the others to leave," Whitman said. "I was afraid that this might happen. He's not disloyal, but he resents my leadership, and the fact that I have placed Amy as my second in command instead of him. I purposely did not introduce you because in the event of your capture, you could not reveal their identities. I sent them away for their own protection. I'm sure that the others understood, but Billy doesn't always keep a cool head. I didn't expect this, though. We may have less time than we thought."

We all looked at each other as a general feeling of dread crept over the room.

"I thought it seemed strange that he was with you," I said, turning to Amy. "Why isn't he in training camp?"

"Billy was rejected for a birth defect. He was born with no left foot. He wears an artificial one, that's why you didn't notice."

Whitman answered, "I suspect that his rejection by the army was his main reason for joining the movement. Like some boys, he expected glory from serving in the military. When he was denied that, he sought to make a mark in another way. Up until recently, he's done fine work for us, but he may think that he'll be hailed a hero if he turns you in."

"Is there anything that we can do?" Mrs. Royce asked.

"I'm going to try and find him," Whitman said. "If nothing else, I can at least buy us some time. Amy, you and Mrs. Royce should stand guard in the woods, but stay out of sight. If the MPs come to check out Billy's story, at least you can warn Andy and Mark." Then turning to us, "How soon can you go?"

"Mark can go at anytime," Andy put in. "But if the MPs come here and damage the time machine, he'll never get back!"

This was becoming a serious development. To return to the past, at exactly the right point in time, and to find and stop Mrs. Royce from alerting the Hessians would be a small miracle. Now, even if the mission were successful, I could be stuck there if the military police found and destroyed the time machine before I returned. Or would there be no MPs if the timeline were restored? Or was it simply that all this happened before, and both Mrs. Royce and I were supposed to go back because it was part of the original history? One thing was certain; we had no time to analyze all this now!

Whitman heard Andy and tried to calm some of his fears. "I'm hoping that Billy didn't tell the military police captain about this. If he did, I'll make sure that he finds me first so I can deny Billy's story. It won't stop an investigation, but it will delay it. I know the captain won't call his superiors unless he's sure. Billy has the reputation of popping off every now and then, and I'm guessing that nobody will believe him–at least at first."

"Do you want me to go with you?" Amy asked. "If two people deny Billy's story, we may be able to stall longer."

"I think it's best if you stay with our friends. They're still new here, and if someone shows up, they'll need your help explaining themselves." With that, Whitman left for town.

Amy had "borrowed" the second coat from a lady at the orphanage, and we gave it the same treatment as the first one. Once it looked sufficiently beat up, I put it on. I couldn't button it, so I left it open and put the larger coat over it. After that, the blanket went on. Amy had brought some gloves from home, but I was afraid that they would look too out of place. Instead, I wrapped rags around my hands and tied the ends about my wrists. My fingers were a little exposed, but I was still better dressed than your average Continental soldier. I always wear T-shirts with pockets, and that's where I put the transmitter.

Amy and Andy gave me the once over and decided that I didn't look anything like a Continental soldier, but I was dirty and gamy and since it would be dark, we hoped that it would be good enough. Andy found some wonderful information in the book that I had brought home from the library. The countersign for Washington's army that night was "Victory or death." My ensemble was complete: Brand new coat, beat up to look old–75 pounds; old blanket trashed to look older–two shillings;

new pants given the same wearing out treatment–2 pounds; disguise and counter sign to pass through Washington's army pickets unmolested–priceless!

Andy's mom gave me a kiss and told me quietly that I was to stop her no matter what it took. Andy shook my hand and gave me a pat on the back. I hugged Amy and lightly kissed her cheek. My eyes were filled with tears, and I couldn't help saying how much I would miss her, and I how truly sorry I was for what I was about to do. She smiled, held my face between her hands, and told me that it had to be this way. When I stepped on the platform, Andy went back to the computer terminal. He motioned to Amy and his mom to move back.

"Mark, I've checked out the transmitter and turned the radio on. How much time will you need there?" Andy asked. I had forgotten about that. I knew that Washington took at least half a day to cross the river and make his way to Trenton. I figured I'd give myself at least that much.

"Twelve hours should do it," I answered.

"Okay, I've set the timer for five minutes, like we talked about, but I won't press the button until you say so, or until twelve hours have passed. If things start to get rough on this end, I'll restore the automatic call back routine and bypass the button. That way you'll come back when the timer runs out even if no one is here. Don't worry about anything on this end, okay? I mean *anything*."

I was nervous and my hands were sweaty, but I nodded that I understood. Andy pointed at Amy and gave the thumbs up sign. He seemed as impressed as I was at the enormous sacrifice that she and Whitman were making. Their peace movement might require them to give up their lives for their cause, but we were asking them to give up their *world*, and they were willing to do it without reservation.

I felt the now familiar tingling and saw the green haze that told me that the disintegration process had begun. I could see everything in Andy's cellar, but I was unable to move. I knew that I would black out soon, and I found myself hoping that I would land in the right place and at the right time. I knew that Andy and his mom were thinking the same thing. I also hoped that I wouldn't land in the Delaware River! All my careful preparations to stay warm would then be lost, and this would turn into a struggle for survival! When I was transported to Gettysburg on my first trip, I woke up in a field at dusk before the third day of the battle. At that time, I was disoriented because I hadn't realized that I had moved through time as well as space. This time I was more confident, and I possessed a clear and distinct goal. Failure, however, would be catastrophic.

I thought about what Andy's mom said to me as I left. She asked me stop her no matter what it took. I had not prepared myself to do anything more than find her, explain what had happened, and assume she'd understand and cooperate. Well, I'd worry about that when the time came, and that was my last thought before I lost consciousness.

# Chapter 17—The Mission Begins

I awoke in the woods at the edge of a river. It was dark out, and fortunately, it didn't look like I had been spotted by anyone. My head ached just as it did on my last transport, and I decided to lie down until it cleared. I didn't hear anything from Andy, but the transmitter was buried under layers of clothing. The wind blew bitter cold, and I was sincerely happy that I hadn't landed in the water. I doubted whether I would have survived the soaking and exposure for very long. I thought about Mrs. Royce and wondered how she held up as long as she did.

After a few minutes, I decided that I'd contact Andy to make sure that the transmitter worked. Andy and I developed a protocol during our last adventure. He doesn't initiate a conversation unless he can hear exactly what's going on. That way, he doesn't give me away to the locals. Usually, he can hear what's going on around me unless, of course, the transmitter is buried under several layers of clothing as it is now. I planned on finding a way to fix that because his input at critical moments is invaluable. In Gettysburg, he was able to help out immensely by giving me very useful historical data. Besides, it's always good to have a second point of view. First things first, I pulled out the transmitter and began speaking.

"Andy, can you hear me?"

"Loud and clear, buddy. Do you have your bearings, yet?"

"Not really, it's darn cold though, so I'll take that as a good sign." I was starting to feel it through everything that I was wearing. On top of that, it was starting to sleet.

"Well here's another good sign. Your transporter coordinates check out okay."

Everything was working out just right so far; this was almost a little too easy. I was struck by a sudden horrible thought. "How accurate are your figures, Andy. I can't tell what side of the river I'm on."

"It's not accurate enough to tell me that. I can pinpoint you within a few hundred yards or so. How close are you to the river bank?"

"Fairly close, a hundred yards maybe."

"The river flows north to south. Go to the edge and watch the ice float by. If it's moving from left to right you're in Pennsylvania, if it's right to left then you're in New Jersey. We'll pray that you're in New Jersey."

"I'm heading to the river bank now." That was why I liked to keep the lines of communication open with Andy. The walk was tough in the underbrush, but there were no leaves on the trees, so visibility was good despite the dark and sleet. I covered the distance in about a minute. The short walk warmed me up, but the rags that I wrapped around my hands in the interest of looking authentic were no substitutes for gloves. I wished that I had brought the pair that Amy offered.

I stood on the riverbank and watched. The ice was plentiful, and as I picked up the motion, my optimism suddenly vanished. The ice flowed from left to right. I was on the Pennsylvania side!

"Andy, I'm in Pennsylvania!" I said, a little more loudly than I had intended. I heard Andy swear on the other end.

"This was going too well," he said. "Can you see any activity on the river? I mean do you have to go north or south to contact the army? You're going to have to cross with them." That was an adventure that I wasn't relishing, but then again, I didn't know any kids who could say they crossed the Delaware River with General Washington! I remembered what I had read that morning in the library. Washington made his crossing about nine miles north, or upstream, of Trenton and then traveled south to attack the town. Since it was totally quiet here, I guessed that I was too far south. I told Andy my plan.

"Both directions look deserted, but if the Continentals were ferrying boats for the crossing, they would likely come from the north to avoid detection. Since I don't see anything going on here, I'm going to head upstream and hope something turns up. Just pray that I don't run out of time."

"Oh we will, Mark, at least the MPs haven't made an appearance here, yet."

I started out and planned my entrance into the Continental army. The sleet was steady, making the trail hard going, but the exercise made me feel better, and just as importantly, it was keeping me warm. In the back of my mind was the constant fear that I may have missed the time window. What if it was December 31, 1776, and the battle had been over for a week, or maybe it was 1810 and it was quiet because the hour was late and there *really was* nothing going on. Even if I was at the right time, being on the wrong side of the river complicated things enormously. No longer could I simply find Andy's mom, stop her from reaching the Hessian outpost, and call Andy to bring us back. Now I would have to get into the Continental army, make the river crossing, escape from the army, and *then* find Mrs. Royce. To further confuse things, I remembered that the road the Continental Army used came to an intersection about five miles from Trenton. The road that continued straight ahead led to the Trenton waterfront; the one to the left led to the opposite end of the town. Andy's mom could have been transported onto either road, and at the moment, it was impossible to tell which! I would never have time to search both roads. If only there was a way to narrow the choice.

"Andy, can your mom hear me?" I asked.

"She's outside on watch, but I can get her."

"I need to ask her some questions."

"Okay." Andy's mom was at the radio in seconds.

"I'm right here, Mark," she answered.

"Do you remember seeing the river when you were walking in the dark?" I asked.

"No. It was snowing pretty hard and visibility was poor, but I *was* looking to both sides trying to find shelter," Mrs. Royce answered.

"Andy, open the book to the map. The main road from the crossing reaches an intersection about five miles above the town. Then it continues straight and bends toward the river. What's the name of that road?"

"I'm way ahead of you. I've torn out everything on the Battle of Trenton and laid it out on the bench, including the map. The road that bends toward the river is–oh, oh, you may need to write this one down, it's tough."

"I'll try to remember," I answered.

"It's called River Road. Think you can handle it?" Actually the humor eased the tension that I'd been feeling since I found out that I was in Pennsylvania.

"Oh, I hope so. What's the other one, the road that goes to the left?" I asked.

"At the intersection it's called Scotch Road, but after about four miles–that's a mile north of town–it merges with Pennington Road. That's the road that Washington took. I'm guessing that you're going that way, too."

"Yes, I'll never be able to check out both roads, and if your mom didn't see the river…"

"I hear you, but what if Mom's on the section of River Road before the intersection?"

"If I begin my search after I cross, then I'll cover that on the way to Trenton anyway. The only decision I'll have to make is at the intersection. It's a guess, I know, but at least it's an educated guess."

"I suppose, but we're beginning to rely an awful lot on luck. I don't have any better ideas, though."

"Someday this will make a great Tom Cruise movie. Mission Impossible X."

We *were* relying a bit too much on luck, but I was warm, loose, and starting to feel pretty good as I trudged on. My exercise high didn't last long because after what seemed liked two or three miles I still saw no sign of the Continental army. I also had no idea what time it was. I knew that the troops began crossing around 6:00 p.m. local time at a place called McKonkey's Ferry. It had been dark for a while now, so I knew it was well past that! What if I was heading in the wrong direction?

The river took a slight westerly bend, and at the point I saw a lone rower beach a dory and pull it ashore. I decided to risk contact and ask where I was. I whistled Dixie as I approached to avoid startling the man. I was also sure that he would not recognize the tune. He looked up, dropped his bowline, and immediately produced a flintlock that he pointed it in my direction. The powder was probably wet and the odds on the gun actually firing were low, but I needed information not a fight. I raised my hands and hailed.

"Don't shoot, sir. I be lookin' fer the ferry." I didn't know the dialect from the Colonial period, and I hoped that I could be understood.

"Come closer, but don't be movin' quick, I say." At least he didn't shoot first and ask questions later. "You with Washington?" Washington! Maybe I was on time after all, but I wasn't out of the woods, yet. My answer to this question could determine whether the mission was a success or failure. Was the boatman a Tory–a colonist who remained loyal to the British? If so, a yes answer could get me killed. I tried a non-answer.

"Who?" I asked.

"Washington! Don' ye kno' who *he* be?" he asked, surprised that I appeared so dumb. I was closer to the man now, but the course change in the conversation seemed to relax him. I decided to press the little advantage that I had. "My daddy took sick in Newark." I pronounced it Noo-ahk. "I have to go thar' to help him. Do ye kno' whar the ferry be." I spoke slowly and that seemed to convince him that I was dim-witted.

"Not McKonkey's Ferry," he said, as though it were a question.

"Yes, McKonkey's. That's the place. I go to Noo-ahk." I was elated! I found someone who knew the place! The next thing he said was even better news.

"Not likely this night. That Rebel, Washington, is all over the place. He stole ever' boat from Port Jervis down ta here. Mor'n three weeks ago it was when them Rebels runned from Jersey. Didn't want the British to use 'em to cross the river and finish off what's lef' o' his sorry army. Well, here's one he ain't gittin'," he said as he kicked the bow of his dory. "Here, lend a hand, laddie."

I helped the man pull his boat off the riverbank and into the woods. He wanted it far out of sight of anyone navigating the bend. His caution made me guess that I was close to my interim destination. I listened, but the wind masked any sound from the north. Looking closely at the man, I saw that he had no teeth, and when he stood, I viewed a physique that was short and stooped. It was obvious that he'd had a hard life. A body could be worn out at thirty by the physical demands of life in the eighteenth century. Because of that, it was impossible to guess his age. From his conversation, it was apparent that the man was a Tory. That was one advantage that the Americans had. It was often very difficult for the British to know just who the enemy was! Generally, the merchants who sold goods from England tended to sympathize with the British, while the yeoman farmers, fishermen, and tradesmen leaned toward the Rebels.

After we covered his boat with evergreen boughs, I decided that it was time to move on.

"Is the McKonkey ferry this way?" I asked, pointing north.

He laughed a loud laugh with his open, toothless mouth. "McKonkey's boats be thar, but I tol' ye. Washington has 'em. He has 'em all. Stole the Durham ore boats from Sussex County, too. Ol' McKonkey ain't got nothin'!"

"Washington has the boats, you say. I'll cross wit' him." I knew I was pushing it, but I needed to know exactly where the Continental Army was. I thought for a moment that I had gone too far.

"Your daddy be a *Rebel*?" he scowled.

"My daddy's sick," I answered.

"No, what *side* he be on?" he pressed again. More dangerous territory, but I was ready.

"He's on *my* side!" I said, as I pointed at my chest and launched into a big, dumb, toothy grin. "My daddy tol' me that he allays be on *my* side." If I pulled this off I vowed to join the drama club when school started in the fall.

The man shook his head. "Well, I guess ye need someone on ye side, that's fer shur. McKonkey's Ferry be up the river where you was headed. It ain't fer. A mile or so I guess. Thankee fer the help and I hope ye makes it. Ye poor dumb kid, I'd cross yer m'sef if I thought I could fool th'army. Them guards is ever'wher by now, an' I'd lose my boat an' we'd both be in jail." With that he shook my hand and went on his way. The encounter was worthwhile. I had found out where the crossing was taking place, and I wasn't far away. More than that, I knew that I wasn't too late! Mrs. Royce had recalled seeing the new day dawning while she trekked through the snow to the farmhouse. I had time, but how much–certainly enough for another call to Andy.

"Andy, did you hear any of that?" I asked after I walked a few hundred feet. I wanted to make sure that I was far enough away from the boatman, but I didn't want to look back to check.

"No, you need to put the transmitter on the outside, maybe just under the blanket. I might be able to hear you then," he replied. I told him that I met a man, a Tory, and I was able to fool him about my identity and get some valuable information.

"I acted like the village idiot! It worked great. The man never suspected a thing."

"I'm glad to hear it. That shouldn't have been much of a stretch for you." I was too happy to even respond to the dig.

"I'm only about a mile from the crossing, and I think I'm early enough! How about that!" I was having trouble controlling my exuberance.

"Awright!" he yelled. "That *is* good news!" Then in the background I heard him yell, "He's found the crossing and he's there in time!" More hooting and hollering. Amy and Mrs. Royce must have been in the cellar.

"Andy, why aren't the women keeping a look out?" I asked.

"They are. Amy came in to eat and was just heading back out. Mom was coming in. Your timing was perfect! What great news." It was indeed great news. Each of us had put all our hopes into the success of this mission. No one dared to think of how it would be if I were to fail. Capture by the military police and death in a British North American prison was the probable fate of Amy, Andy, and Mrs. Royce. The same would happen to me if I returned; otherwise, I'd be marooned or killed in the eighteenth century. These were not exactly prosperous career paths, and the sense of relief that we were experiencing was understandable. We discovered that we'd just crossed two great hurdles. I managed to find my way to the right place, the point of crossing, and just as important, I arrived before Mrs. Royce changed history!

However, we still had a long way to go.

# Chapter 18–Crossing The Delaware

After walking a few more minutes, I could see Washington's army crossing the river. The sleet had turned to snow, and the ground had become very slippery. I fell twice when I stepped on stones that were encased in ice. I kept to the woods and hoped that I could slip into the army somewhere near the front so that I could cross with the next group. I stopped for a moment to watch the scene. The boats being used were of assorted sizes. The smaller boats ferried men only, and I gathered that they were the ones that were commandeered from the local watermen. The main boats, carrying men and some war materiel, were large, approximately forty feet long and eight feet deep, and used either four or five oarsmen. Some men used poles to push the boats forward. I realized at once that these were the Durham boats that the old waterman spoke of.

The opposite bank didn't look very far away, maybe three hundred yards, but everything seemed to move very slowly. It was impossible to see how many boats were used in the dark, but the whole thing reminded me of ants moving back and forth between the hive and some kid's dropped lollypop. Ice chunks partially clogged the river, and the oarsmen frequently cursed as the miniature bergs thudded against the boats. I knew that I should keep moving, but I figured I give Andy one last call before I made my attempt to enlist.

"Andy, any details that you can tell me concerning this trip would be helpful. I know the general stuff well enough."

"I'm glad you called. I found a few things that you might be able to use. The man in charge of getting everyone and everything over to the east bank of the river is Colonel Henry Knox."

"The same guy that Fort Knox is named after?" I asked.

"The very one. He's also the guy that supervised the movement of the cannon from Fort Ticonderoga to Boston to relieve the siege on that city earlier in the war. Washington trusts him to do a good job. He won't be hard to find. It says here that he's six-foot-three and weighs two hundred and eighty pounds!"

"Wow, you're right! I should be able to spot him very easily." The average man of the eighteenth century was considerably smaller than his twenty-first-century counterpart. While a man the size of Colonel Knox may be large by our standards, he would be a Goliath to his contemporaries. "Anything else?" I asked.

"Seamen from Marblehead, Massachusetts are rowing the boats. Colonel John Glover commands them. I don't have a description of him. Washington credits those guys with saving his army during the retreat from Long Island the previous summer, so he trusts him.

"The last boat reaches the New Jersey shore around 3:00 a.m. December 26. Washington crosses with Knox some time before that. If you can't find Knox on the west bank, it's a safe bet that both he and Washington have gone across. If you can estimate how many troops are still on your side, maybe you can guess the time."

"Wouldn't it be easier to ask someone?"

"I wouldn't try that. Those guys won't have watches. They may think that you're weird or something."

I had forgotten about that. Knowing the precise hour didn't become important to the general population until the industrial revolution got rolling. Only when large numbers of people began to work shifts in the factories and offices did knowing the precise minutes and hours of the day begin to take on significance. Washington and his officers would certainly have watches, but it was doubtful that many of the foot soldiers did.

Anyway, I was planning to remain an observer as long as possible, so I didn't see any sense in calling attention to myself.

"Okay, that sounds sensible. I'm heading in. Anything else?"

"Only this: *Be careful.* There's still a long way to go on this mission, but you've done great so far."

"Thanks, I will."

I stopped for a moment, covered the transmitter with my blanket, and walked back down to the riverbank. I covered the last few yards along the water's edge. I was surprised to see that I'd made it all the way to the loading point before I was noticed. A skinny guard leveled a bayoneted musket at me and issued the challenge. "Stop it thar' now, big feller, give us the counter sign." The man was short, dressed in rags, and sported a stubbly beard. I guessed that he wasn't much older than I, and although considerable smaller, I had no intention of taking him on. It was time for the village idiot to emerge once again.

"Victory or death," I offered immediately.

"Where you commin' from. Ain't nobody suppos'd ta be down thar'."

I already had a plan for this one. "I had ta *go*," I said as I grinned and nodded like an idiot. I walked forward and stood directly in front of him. I made sure that the distance between us was uncomfortably close. Since he was supposed to be watching the riverbank, he had to keep looking around me. I could see in the guard's face that he felt very uncomfortable with this. I hoped that he would just tell me to pass, but once again I was disappointed.

"Ye had to go whar'?" he asked while still looking down the river.

"I had ta go *here*!" I said as I turned around and pointed at my rear end.

"Oh, jayses," he replied, "I didn't see ye pass me." I hung my head down and sniveled.

"I got lost," I said as I started shuffling my feet. "Ye ain't gonna tell no one are ye. The boys'll tease me terrible. They tease me terrible all-a-time." I sniffled again.

"No, I reckon not," he said in a tone of genuine sympathy. "Do ye know where ye comp'ny be?" The idiot routine worked again, but I felt a little guilty this time.

"Afixin' ta cross by now," I answered.

"Well, the crossin's just past them supplies, yonder," he said as he pointed in the general direction that I'd been heading.

"Thankee, thankee for not tellin' on me," I gushed, and before he could change his mind, I set out and never looked back.

I found the crossing point easily, and after a few seconds more, I found myself walking by an artillery piece. A genuine eighteenth-century cannon! I stopped for a moment to look it over. The barrel was covered with snow. The wooden chassis was well built and solid. It seemed small, but I felt quite sure that it performed its function just fine. I'd seen Revolutionary-era cannon before in museums, but they were clearly broken down versions of the real thing. I unraveled the rag from my left hand and rubbed the barrel. The iron felt smooth and cold. I realized that I still hadn't thought of a way to bluff my way into the army and make it across the river, and I felt that this was as good a place as any to stop and think.

I leaned against the piece and looked around for Colonel Knox. I couldn't find him anywhere. I figured that both he and Washington must have crossed the river by now. But what should *I* do? I *could* just walk onto a boat with a group of soldiers and hope they didn't ask too many questions, but if I were found out, the game would be up. Maybe if I were bold enough and acted like I belonged there, then perhaps I could pull it off. I'm not sure how long I remained lost in this thought, but I was interrupted by a yell directed at me from a mounted officer. Apparently it wasn't the first time that he shouted in my direction, but it was the first that I heard.

"Well are ye deaf, boy?" he asked. "We're movin' this here artillery piece next. Are you in or not?"

I was shaken out of my trance, and I said the first thing that came to mind. "Victory or death." I realized instantly that wasn't what the officer was looking for.

"Right 'Victory or death,'" the officer said, then to some men nearby, "ahoy lads, give this daft sot a hand loadin' his cannon on t' the barge. I ain't havin' his like muckin' up the works on this night." Then to me again he asked, "Whar be the rest of ye boys, anyway?"

What an opportunity! I didn't need a plan after all. I was getting a free ride! I thought quickly this time. "Yonder sir," I said as I pointed to the rear of the mass of men that had converged on the crossing point, "said they'd be here soon, but I ain't seed 'em. That be a fer time back o' course, sir!"

"Well we ain't got time for that. Get this rig loaded and be darn quick about it."

In less than a minute four teamsters had loaded the cannon, and several horses, onto a flat-bottomed barge. Other equipage was already stowed. The barge was wide and I guessed it to be about thirty to forty feet long. A platform extended out over the water from both the stern and bow. Several soldiers were aboard and the Marbleheaders were about to cast off. I jumped onto the platform seconds before we pulled away.

As I made my way into the barge, I kept looking back, half expecting the officer to find the true owners of the cannon and call me back to face a firing squad. But more than likely, he would be far too busy to give me a thought. It didn't matter. I was crossing the Delaware!

The wind over the open water cut through my clothes and froze me to the bone. This was compounded by the fact that we had to sit still. The other men in the boat felt the same. Some tried to doze, but most of us just shivered and looked miserable. I knew that I was covered better than most, but somehow that knowledge didn't seem to help. At least no one was paying any attention to me, and for that I was grateful.

Our barge was much like the others; we had five men poling. Next to us was a Durham boat filled with soldiers. In it, four men rowed while another manned the tiller. These fellows were having a hard time of it! The floating ice banged the boat frequently, but it was the floes that hit the oars that gave rise to great oaths from the rowers. It would be a long night for the men providing the motive force to bring the Continental army across, but I found myself envious of them. At least the rowing kept them warm. I consciously took a long look around somewhere near the middle of the river. I mustered up as much concentration as possible so as to burn the impressions of what I saw into my memory. No one from my time would ever see the sight of our national army crossing water in rowboats and barges!

I instantly recalled that famous painting, *Washington Crossing the Delaware*, and I was struck by the realization of how historically inaccurate it really was! In the painting, the general was standing in the front of the boat, next to the Stars and Stripes, under a breaking dawn sky. Apparently, it was the artist's romantic notion of what the commander-in-chief should have looked like on this momentous occasion. Instead, he almost certainly sat near the back of a Durham boat, hunched over, trying to stay warm like the rest of us. We also know that he crossed in the middle of the night, and the Stars and Stripes flag hadn't even been designed yet! Heck, I even remember seeing a book about the Battle of Trenton with that painting on the cover. You'd think that an author, writing a period piece, would strive to be more accurate!

Anyway, the visibility was poor, and the snow was coming down harder now, but the river was a beehive of activity. I couldn't help feeling that if this were a clear night, a Hessian patrol would almost certainly have spotted us and spoiled Washington's surprise. Luck was certainly on his side. So far I felt that it was on mine as well. It took about twenty minutes from the time we left Pennsylvania until we were on the east bank. I had made it to New Jersey!

# Chapter 19—Washington And Knox

Soldiers, equipment, cannon, and horses overflowed the landing area and spilled into the woods. Several men were collected and ordered to help lift the cannon off the boat that I took. Once emptied, the vessel was immediately sent back for the next load. Officers and men seemed to be running everywhere. The site looked like bedlam, but order was underneath the chaotic surface. My artillery piece was immediately placed in line with the others for the trip to Trenton. Infantrymen were moved in groups and setup on the road or in the woods in preparation for the march. Only one road was visible, and it headed directly into the woods away from the river. "Road" was a generous term for the path that the army planned to take to Trenton. It was wide enough to accommodate a cannon or a team of horses, and it would have to do. I chuckled when I thought of how quickly this battle, or the whole Revolution for that matter, could be ended by the addition of one Sherman tank!

I looked ahead to see if I could spot the head of the column as it lined up on the road. I figured that they would be the men that led the army to Trenton. Since I couldn't see far from where I was, I moved to a small hill to get a better vantage point. From there I managed to see a few yards farther. The column extended beyond. From the sheer numbers on this side, I guessed that the crossing was well over halfway done.

The road ahead was jammed with soldiers. If I were going to reach the head of the column, I'd have to head into the woods and inch my way through the brush parallel to the road. I was just about to do exactly that when I turned once more toward the river. Two men, walking deliberately up the slope toward me, blocked my field of vision. I froze when I made eye contact with the larger man. He registered no recognition and turned to look at his companion. When both men reached the hilltop, not ten feet from me, they abruptly turned around and faced the river. There was no mistaking them! The larger man was Colonel Knox and the second man–tall but not as wide–had to be General Washington himself! They paid no attention to me. In fact, I don't think they even knew that I was right behind them. I slipped the blanket off my shoulder to allow the transmitter a clear shot and hoped that Andy was nearby.

"You're doing a fine job of this, Henry, but I fear that we will lose our darkness by the time we reach Trenton. Is there any way that we can speed this up?" General Washington asked.

"It's the snow and the river ice, sir, that are slowing us down. I'm afraid we still have two hours to go, General," Colonel Knox replied.

"That'll put us at 3:00 a.m. With five hours march before us, we'll be fighting Hessians in daylight. Mighty hard to surprise them then."

"There's still time to turn back, sir. Call off the attack…"

"I *can't*, Henry," Washington cut him off. "The enlistments for most of these men run out at the end of the year. That's *next week*! We need *victory*, Henry, *victory*! And we need the Hessians' supplies to sustain the army through the winter. This isn't just another battle. It's victory or death for this country. Tonight. With victory, maybe we can convince these veterans to stay on! We *need* these men, Henry," he held his hand out to the men in his front, "or the cause is lost! I owe them my best effort. *All* of us do."

"I understand, sir. The crossing will be made, and I'll do what I can to hurry it along," Colonel Knox added.

The general continued in what sounded to me to be a very kind but tired voice, "And Henry, please tell Generals Sullivan and Greene that I need to see them. If the Hessians know we're coming, we're in for a tough fight."

"Yes sir," Knox answered quietly as he saluted and left. Washington lingered for a few minutes. It was apparent from his conversation with Knox that he was keenly aware that everything was riding on his actions and those of his army tonight. I could only imagine what he must have been feeling as he looked across the river and realized that this army, his beloved men, would be fighting professional Hessian soldiers in broad daylight! I understood now that he had no choice, but what happened in these next hours would determine the fate of the Republic and the fate of the world. I had to offer what I could.

"General?" My voice cracked as I said the word, and my knees felt rubbery when he turned around. For a second I thought that maybe I was going to end up in the stockade, but he looked me over and smiled.

"Yes sir?" he asked. General Washington called me "sir." I was pumped! Andy *had* to get that on tape!

"Well, General, you don't need ta worry is all. We're gonna win today," I started. "I get these feelings, General, like I know what's gonna happen 'fore it does. My ma calls it the gift. It don't come too often, mind you, but it ain't never wrong. I got it today. We're gonna win awright and most o' the boys, they'll re-up afta. And someday, them Redcoats'll go home. I just know it, sir."

"Well, I thank you, son, for your encouragement." Then he winked as he continued, "I think we're going to win, too. What's your name, lad?"

"Mark Walton, sir," I said as I saluted.

"Well, Mr. Walton, God speed to us both."

I smiled as I gave a second salute and walked as deliberately as I could into the woods. I knew I couldn't fail now. I'd promised General George Washington himself that we would win!

# Chapter 20–A Walk In The Woods

My step was light and I felt great as started my hike into the woods. Yep, it's the drama club for sure when school starts in the fall. My idea was to get upriver and trudge through the woods parallel to the road. If all went well, I'd pass the army, get back on the road, and start my search for Mrs. Royce. But the underbrush was thick, and it didn't take me long to figure out that I was in for hard trip. I was alone, so I figured that this was a great time to call Andy.

"Andy, I met Washington!" I was still very excited. "I even talked to him! It was great!"

"I heard the whole thing and couldn't believe my ears! I almost yelled right out loud when I heard him answer you. I'm going to nominate you for an Academy Award when this is over."

We laughed a little more over this, but I wanted some information. "I got a time fix, too. Washington said that it will be 3:00 a.m. in two hours. That puts the time at 1:00 a.m. now. I'm in the woods working my way to the front of the column. I'm guessing that it's going to take about an hour. Do you have any more history that you can pass on to me?" I asked.

"The army marches from the landing site to Bear Tavern–about a mile. Then they turn right onto the upper portion of River Road and march three more miles to the intersection. Washington sets up his command in two divisions. The first division is in the very front and is commanded by General John Sullivan. The second division is next and is commanded by

General Nathanael Greene. When the army reaches the intersection, Sullivan and the first division will continue straight on River Road and attack Trenton by the riverfront. Greene's division will turn left onto the Scotch Road and attack the town from the opposite side."

"Okay, I've got that," I said. "I remember reading that in the library, but I appreciate the reminder."

"Here's something else," Andy added. "There's a captain commanding a New York artillery company that you should know. His name is Alexander Hamilton. He's with Greene's reserves, so he may not be too far up the road just yet."

"That's good to know," I said. "It may come in handy if someone stops me."

Andy continued, "Washington's new timetable is right on. The battle starts somewhere around 8:00 a.m., that's about seven hours away. I'm guessing that Mom tipped them off sometime near 6:00 a.m. if it was starting to get light. It might be later than that, though. The Hessians wouldn't need much warning."

"Gotcha. I think that if I can get past the head of the column by 3:00 a.m. I'll be okay. That's when the Continental army moves isn't it?"

"It's near that time. They finish crossing somewhere around 3:00 a.m. I think they actually move out around 4:00 a.m. Also, this may be useful, the commander of the Hessians is a colonel named Johann Rall. He's considered a great hero in British North America of course," Andy added.

"From what I remember from school history, he's probably very drunk by now. In fact, that's what made Washington's plan work, the blizzard, and the fact that some of the Hessian officers were hammered. They also didn't think they needed to send out any patrols in the snow," I said.

"You're probably right, but as you may guess, there's no mention of that in here."

"No, there wouldn't be."

"I don't have anything on the layout of the battlefield. In this book, the Hessians trap both Greene's and Sullivan's troops on the roads and push them back to the river. That's not going to happen tonight."

"Damn straight," I said, and I meant it. "I remember from history class that the Americans set up the artillery to fire along the main roads. Once the Hessians were knocked off balance, Greene's and Sullivan's infantry surrounded the town." I was getting ahead of myself and Andy saw it.

"Hey, hey, Napoleon. You're there to stop Mom from warning the Hessians. *That's all!* Washington did a fine job of fighting the battle without you last time, remember?" Andy said.

*Or am I here every time the battle is fought?* I thought grimly. The old paradox was playing itself out again. Am I supposed to do something that causes the Continental army to win tonight, or do they win in spite of me? I already spoke to the general. Did I convince him to continue when later he may have decided on his own to turn back? Am I nothing more than an element of danger that could explode like a loose cannon and change the timeline in such a way that neither the United States nor British North America ever existed? Whatever it was, there was no way that I could solve the puzzle now. I decided that I'd do what I did at Gettysburg. Follow my instincts and hope for the best.

"Okay, I get it. I'll find your mom and let you know so you can bring us back," I answered. "How's everything going on your end?"

"Okay so far. Mom and Amy are keeping a look out, but no sign of either Whitman or that Billy Hudson kid, yet. I can lock the cellar door at a moment's notice, and there's plenty of heavy stuff to use as a barricade if I need to buy time. Amy doesn't think anything's going to happen, but she's planning to run the same interference that Whitman mentioned if the MPs show up. Time might be critical then."

The mention of Amy put a lump in my throat. She was so brave. I vowed that if we were successful, I would honor her memory for the rest of my life. I pulled myself together to close with Andy.

"Okay, I better get started. I'll call again when I can." I signed off and set out for the front.

# Chapter 21–The Road To Bear Tavern

"Who is that cluck out there in the woods!" An officer called in my direction! He kept his voice down, but the meaning was clear–I was caught! I didn't get far enough into the woods and now someone spotted me. I didn't know what to do. I kept moving hoping that he'd forget I was there. He didn't. "Hey, you stupid sot. Get in here or I'll have you bayoneted!" I was trapped! I could run and get away, but I'd be heading in the opposite direction from Trenton, and I'd lose all hope of finding Mrs. Royce. I had the countersign, so I figured I'd take my chances with the officer. I waved and headed over.

"Countersign," the officer said with a cold stare.

"Victory or death," I answered, glad again that I had found that little piece of information.

"What were you doing out there? You wouldn't be thinking of deserting, now? We shoot deserters."

"No, sir," I said with a salute. "Nature's latrine, then I got lost." It worked before so I figured that I'd stick with it. No tough guy's ever going to check your drawers to see if you were lying. "I been sick, sir, and crossed late. I'm tryin' ta fin' my comp'ny."

The officer smirked. "What company you with?"

I answered the first thing that came to mind, "The New York Artillery, sir."

"Well that explains why you don't have a musket. Well, I don't know where they are, so join this here line. If we find your company you can rejoin them. Be sharp now." The man motioned for me to fall in and I complied. I had no choice. Fortunately, the man left a few minutes later. Whew! That was close! My heart was racing and I was sure that I looked sick. Maybe that was what saved me.

"New York Artillery, ye say," the soldier next to me said. I was still breathing hard when I nodded. "I think them fellers be up just a piece. Hundert yards, mebbe less. You don't look so good, though. You okay?"

"Thanks," I said, "I'm okay. I was sick afore. I'll rest here a minute. Then maybe I'll look."

I smiled and he grinned back. "I reckon, we all been thar afore," he said with genuine sympathy. Several of his comrades murmured agreement.

I looked closely at the man. I guessed that he was a little older than I and dressed as shabbily as his fellows. I wasn't sure if it was the physical activity of the march or the adrenaline rush that comes from knowing you're about to get into a fight, but none of the men seemed cold. I wasn't either, but underneath my shabby coat were more layers of clothing. I made sure that my blanket covered everything. I didn't want the boys to decide that I was too comfortable and feel inclined to relieve me of the coat that I was saving for Mrs. Royce. I was also happy that the snow covered my Nikes, since they would never pass for Colonial era footwear. As we waited, I recalled what General Washington said about the men's enlistments. Many were scheduled to run out within a week, and he needed a victory to give the men hope and help his re-enlistment drive. I figured I'd find out from the soldiers first hand what it was all about.

"Ye fixin' ta go home afta this here battle t'nite?" I asked. I wasn't comfortable with the accent I had been using, but I couldn't think of anything else. The soldier didn't seem to notice or care.

"Depends on what happ'ns, I reckon. If we lose and I ain't dead, I'll prolly go home. Iff'n we win and git good vittles, I be figur'n on stayin'. I don't like quittin', but a man gotta eat, don't he?" he answered.

"Well, I'm goin' home anyway," the man behind him said. "I had nuff o' this marchin' and freezin'. I'm goin' home at midnight on New Year's Eve!"

"No you ain't," another man broke in. "You'll miss us and be back in a week. I know I ain't goin' home, yit. I wants ta see how it ends."

"You'd better hope it don' end wiff ye dead," still another man added. "We ain't burying your sorry arse in this here frozen ground. But I'm wiff Sam, here. I'm leavin' iff'n we git licked agin."

This banter went on for some time. It wasn't exactly a statistically correct poll, but it seemed that Washington was right. He needed a victory or he was in danger of losing his army when the enlistments ran out. I found myself hoping that the Hessians had a good food supply to help Washington convince the men to stay on! I was daydreaming about that when the soldier I first met in the line poked me.

"Well, what about you? You staying?" he asked.

"I reckon to stay iff'n we win. If we don't, I may go home, too." I took the safe answer. A general murmur of agreement followed, and again the line went silent as we waited. The snow was getting heavier, and I knew that we must be nearing the marching hour. All this time we'd been inching forward, and I think in total we moved a hundred yards, but now the column stopped. Nobody was talking now. In fact, I suspected that a good many of the men were asleep standing up. One man actually tipped over in the snow, and his comrades had to shake him awake!

While this had been going on, I formulated a plan to leave the group and begin my search for Andy's mom. I knew that I was running out of time, and I still didn't know her location. I was going to need some help. I thought about this for a while and came up with a bold plan to enlist a few of my new comrades to aid in the search. First, I needed to get away so that I could move more freely.

"I'm goin' up ta find my company. Where'd ye say it was agin," I asked.

"Yonder, 'bout a hundert yards, if they been movin' like us."

"Thanks," I said, and I quietly edged out into the woods. My idea was to move through the woods next to the column until I reached the artillery. I was foiled almost immediately.

"You thar! Where ye think ye be goin'?" someone shouted. It may have been the company sergeant; it wasn't the officer from earlier.

"I havta go…" I began and immediately started making puking noises. "I hav…." I faked another puke.

"Go on then but be quick about it," he yelled out. I kept moving, but I distinctly heard my former comrade note that my bowels would "prolly" kill me before the Hessians did! It wasn't long before I was out of sight and working my way "up yonder." Plan A wasn't smooth, but I made it. When I guessed that I moved the estimated distance, and I spied a pair of artillery pieces, I figured it was time to execute plan B.

"MESSAGE FOR GENERAL GREENE FROM GENERAL WASHINGTON!" I yelled waving my hand in the air. "MESSAGE FOR GENERAL GREENE FROM GENERAL WASHINGTON!" I repeated. An officer responded instantly.

"*Find out who that is and shut the fool up*!" he said. It wasn't exactly the response that I hoped for, but at least I got noticed. I stopped yelling, but I kept waving my arms. The officer ran over at once. His uniform was sharp, and he looked at me with piercing blue eyes.

"You idiot! This is a surprise attack. Shut up!" He was clearly irate, but he couldn't yell, either.

"A message from General Washington for General Greene, sir," I said as I saluted.

"I know that much, Private. The whole army and probably the Hessians know that, too! What *is* it?"

"I'm sorry, sir, but I was told by the general himself that I was to deliver it to him personally–or Captain Hamilton, sir." I kept my voice low and spoke in my best parochial school grammar. I tried my best to make no facial expressions, either.

"*I'm* Captain Hamilton," he said. "Now *give* me the message, and I'll see that General Greene is *informed*." I could see that he was losing patience. "Now Mister or I'll *shoot* you where you *stand*!" With that he pulled his pistol from inside his coat and aimed it between my eyes! I was dumbfounded and scared to death. He pulled the hammer back with his thumb. I wanted to run but I knew that he'd shoot me for sure if I did. He didn't seem to care that the sound of the shot would have been a lot louder than my voice. I think he *wanted* to do it, and I still couldn't speak. I bowed my head to look at the ground, and I felt as though I was outside of my body watching the last few seconds. Finally a voice.

"The orders are verbal, sir. The general didn't have anything to write on, and he said that it couldn't wait. He dispatched me immediately to find you. If you would be so kind, sir, I will tell you the orders but in a more private setting." I heard the words, but they didn't come from my mouth! I was still feeling stunned from looking down the barrel of Captain Hamilton's pistol! I looked up and saw that the captain appeared to relax, and more importantly, he put the gun away. As he did, my head started to clear. With a shock I realized what had happened. It was Andy! He heard the whole thing! He must have realized that I was in trouble and spoke up! I made a mental note to thank him for that later. And it told me that the military police had not arrested him yet.

Alexander Hamilton was short and slim with curly, brown hair. That is to say, short for someone in my own time. He was of an average height here in 1776. Although I was much taller, he took no notice. In fact he had an air about him that said one thing–confidence. The captain and I walked a short way into the woods. He turned his steely eyes on me once again when he turned to face me in the snow.

"What are these orders, man? And speed up your tongue." This was a guy who got right to the point.

"Scouts have reported to General Washington that a woman was observed walking down the Scotch Road. She appeared to be deranged and fairly naked, sir. The general has ordered me to go ahead and find her.

He fears that she may be a spy and is off to warn the Hessians, sir." I wasn't at all sure that I was taking the right approach, but it was too late to recall my words now.

"That's interesting, Private. How do I know that you, yourself, are not a spy who is merely fabricating a story for safe passage through the line?" he asked with the same stern look that froze me earlier. I had planned this part, and right now, I was relieved that I did.

I smiled my widest grin and said, "The general said that you were intelligent and would not honor such a request without proof." I paused for a moment to let my made-up flattery sink in. "He was unable to provide me with proof. However, he did suggest that you send four of your best men with me. They can keep an eye on me while we search, and we'll rejoin you when we find the woman. As you see, I am unarmed, and I'm temporarily assigned to your command."

"This woman, why didn't the scouts capture her themselves?" Hamilton asked. It was a good question and I was unprepared.

"I'm sorry, sir, I didn't hear you," I stalled.

"I said, why didn't the scouts pick up this woman when they saw her?" he repeated. I tried another non-answer.

"I wouldn't know, sir. The general didn't fill me in on the details. He issued the order and I came as quickly as I could, sir." I hoped that it was enough.

"What is your name?"

"Mark Walton," I answered.

"Well, Mr. Walton, be assured that if we do not find this woman, you will be placed under arrest until I can verify your story with the general. He'd better have sent you, or I'll watch you swing at the end of a rope!" From the look in his eye, I knew that he meant it. "Come with me and I'll find you four men."

Whew! A close one, but I got the help that I needed. I felt that I had to add one more thing. "Captain, the general ordered that the woman not be harmed. She's to be covered and kept warm so that she can be questioned." If he heard me, he didn't acknowledge it. Captain Hamilton was thinking, and as he did, he stroked one of the cannon as though it were a favorite pet. This may be the era of flintlocks, powder horns, and lances, but artillery was king.

"*Sergeant Milbury*!" It wasn't quite a yell, but it got the desired result. Word was quickly passed down the line until a soldier suddenly appeared.

"Yes, sir," he said as he saluted.

"Sergeant, I want you to pick three men for special duty. You and your men are to accompany Private Walton here to search for a half-naked woman walking in the snow."

"Sir?" The sergeant was clearly puzzled.

"Mr. Walton here says that he comes from General Washington himself with orders to find this woman and clothe her. We are not equipped to handle women prisoners at the moment, so it should suffice to stow her someplace where we can pick her up later. Is that clear, Sergeant?"

"Yes, sir, but begging the captain's pardon, why do we need five men?" The sergeant understood, but he was still confused about something.

"Good question, Sergeant. You and your men will be searching for the woman but also watching Private Walton here," he pointed at me. "I'm not entirely convinced of his story, but the exercise will give you and your men a better idea of the lay of the land. Also, you are to go to the outskirts of the town. If you do not find the woman, place Private Walton under arrest and bring him to me. If he attempts to escape or cry out, kill him on the spot."

"Yes, sir," he said, and as he saluted the captain, he shot a look of suspicion in my direction.

"Sergeant, see if you can find a blanket or something to cover the woman," Hamilton said.

"No need, Captain. General Washington gave me this for the purpose," I said as I opened my overcoat to reveal the worn coat that Amy had given me. This had a good effect. Everyone in that army knew that there wasn't a spare coat, or blanket, or rag to be had. If I possessed one, then it came from some high level. The sergeant was clearly impressed. His doubts seemed to be removed at once, but if Captain Alexander Hamilton had changed his opinion of me, then his face didn't show it.

"One last thing, Sergeant. Be sure you're back with us when we prepare to take the town. I aim to win today, and these cannon are going to make that happen." It was clear that Captain Hamilton was also an ambitious man. The look in his eye told it all. He considered the artillery's role in this battle to be paramount, and himself the luckiest man alive to be with it. Despite his obvious snootiness, I found that I liked the man, and I was very glad, at this moment, that he was on our side!

# Chapter 22–The Search Is On!

It took only a few minutes to round up the other three men, and together we set off down the road. I was afraid at first that I was going to be led at the point of a bayonet and gutted if we didn't find Andy's mom, so I was happy to observe that the sergeant seemed to cut me some slack since the episode with the coat. Nevertheless, he was a professional, and even if he regarded me with less suspicion, he was still determined to make sure that I stayed in his sights. We traveled in a formation that allowed us to effectively search the area and ensure that I could not run off on my own. In effect, I was surrounded as I marched down the middle of the road. Ten yards in front of me–also in the middle of the road–was a private that the sergeant referred to simply as Gil. On my right, off the edge of the road and a little into the woods, was another private whose name I missed when I was introduced. On my left, also slightly off the road, was a fellow named Jake, while Sergeant Milbury marched about ten yards behind me. The snow was falling at about the same rate as before, and visibility was very poor. Finding Andy's mom was not going to be easy, and it was a long way to Trenton. I hoped for more luck.

After we'd walked about an hour with no sign of Mrs. Royce, I began to get an uneasy feeling in my gut. The same old doubts began to creep into my head. What if I didn't find her? What if we got stuck here? What if something else went wrong? I desperately wanted to talk with Andy, but unless we broke our formation, there was no chance of that.

We reached the intersection and I instructed the sergeant to take the left onto the Scotch Road. We continued along this route another hour and still saw nothing. Suddenly, the man out in front stopped and held up one hand. Everyone but the sergeant stopped in his tracks. Could this be it! Did the man spot her? The sergeant passed me and slowly made his way to the leader. Just as he got there, a deer bounded across the road. A false alarm. No Mrs. Royce. What time was it? We had to be nearing the hour that Andy's mom said that she walked to the farmhouse and met the Hessians.

I began to develop a sinking feeling that we weren't going to make it. I imagined Andy sitting in front of the receiver waiting for any sign that his mother had been found. It had to be hard for him. At least I could actively search while Andy could only wait and hope. All he could hear was the steady sound of footfalls in the snow. It may be that he couldn't even hear that, a cruel plight to be sure.

A few more minutes passed. My heart was racing. The army had to have left Bear Tavern and started the march to Trenton by now. How far behind us were they? During the walk I had developed the habit of squinting through the snow. Was it getting lighter? The visibility was still poor. Was there something ahead? I looked closer, concentrating on the image. It was an outline, big and dim, but a farmhouse for sure–and a barn around the back! There! On the right side of the road! But where was Mrs. Royce? Were we too late? Was this the right house? I kept looking. Concentrating. I heard the man in front of me scuffing the ground. Why wasn't I aware of that sound before? I had to risk calling Andy. He had to know if we were failing. If someone heard me, I'd just have to explain it away.

"Andy, nothing yet. Can you here me?" I whispered. I knew that he'd be right at the receiver if he hadn't been captured.

"Mark! Oh man! Billy Hudson's bringing the MPs here! They're at the street. No sign of Whitman, either. He must be in jail. Amy is getting ready to head them off. Have you found my mom?" Andy sounded desperate. We both knew that this could be the end. A jail cell for Andy, his mom, and Amy and…"Mark, if the situation looks hopeless here, I'll shutdown the time machine. You're better off not coming back."

"No! Wait! I want to be with you, and Amy, and your mom. You're all the family I have now!"

"You can't; you'll die in jail here. At least there you'll have a chance."

"No, don't…Hang on…" I had nothing, but I didn't want to let go. I squinted into the snow. I saw motion ahead, and then I heard it! Someone was pounding on the farmhouse door! Gil, the man in front, stopped and raised his hand again. I pointed to the farmhouse as the sergeant came up to me.

"That's her!" I whispered to the sergeant, but loud enough for Andy to hear. At least I hoped that he heard. I whispered to the sergeant again, "On the porch. Hessians are in the house. We've got to stop her before they wake up! If they alert the main army at Trenton we're sunk!" Then into the transmitter, "Andy we've found her." But I heard no reply.

Sergeant Milbury was a man of action; I'll give him that. He sprang into a full run immediately. "Hurry men, stop her now!" he ordered and bolted for the porch. I heard the pounding on the door again as I started to sprint. I caught the sergeant in three strides. In five, I caught Gil. In ten, I was on the porch stripping off my coat and putting it around Mrs. Royce. She had slumped down to the floor. As I was pulling Andy's mom away, the door opened. The Hessians were awake!

The rest seemed like a blur. A figure charged passed me and dove through the open door with his bayoneted rifle directly in front. I found out later that it was Gil. The unsuspecting Hessian never knew what hit him. I remember seeing both figures fall. Gil slid across the floor and hit the wall on the other side. The Hessian lay flat on his back on the floor. The rifle was still attached to the bayonet and seemed to rise vertically out of the fallen Hessian's chest. He was impaled to the floor! Blood seemed to flow everywhere. The Hessian shook in a death rattle and went limp. His dead eyes were staring at the ceiling! Mrs. Royce opened her mouth to scream, but no sound came out. Before she could try again, I covered her mouth with my hand. The sergeant went in next. He slipped on the blood but managed to stay on his feet. He turned to the right and lunged out of my view. I heard a brief struggle as the third Continental soldier entered the house. Moments later the sergeant was up looking around.

I stopped the no-named man at the doorway and told him to cover the back. He looked at the sergeant who nodded his head. The no-named man sprinted around the corner. This was unbelievable! A full minute couldn't have passed since the time we spotted Andy's mom. Now, two men lay dead, and the floor was slick with blood!

"There's at least two more in the house. Remember, no shooting, no noise," I told the sergeant. "I'll tie her up in the barn." He nodded and quietly started up the stairs. Jake followed. Gil was checking out the downstairs. I started to drag Mrs. Royce toward the barn. She was shivering, and she began to struggle. I was amazed at how strong she was. I knew that I had to identify myself, or she was going to get away. I heard a man upstairs cry out in German.

"Mrs. Royce, it's me! Mark!" I said, but her eyes showed no recognition. "Mrs. Royce, please stop. I'm here to help you. It's Mark! Mark Walton!" She seemed to calm down a little as she looked at me. I smiled in an attempt to relax her. "It's okay. I'll explain it all later, but you've got to be quiet. The men you saw, they're here to help us. They gave you the coat. Do you understand?" I felt her nod, so I loosened my grip. She opened her mouth wide, and for I moment, I thought that she was going to scream, but she was only flexing her jaw.

"Mark, what is all this?" she whispered. "I'm freezing. How did I get here? Who are those men? Where's Andy?"

"Mrs. Royce, please walk while I tell you." I heard more scuffling noises coming from inside the house. The barn was behind the house and down a slight hill. "Andy's at home, safe and sound," I lied. "Do you remember what you were doing before you ended up–here."

"I was walking through a blizzard…"

"No, Mrs. Royce, at your house, before you landed in this winter wonderland." We were getting near the barn. I had to make her understand before the Continental soldiers came down to get me.

"I don't know…I was going down the stairs and into the cellar…" She was disoriented, but she was gamely fighting for control. "I heard something. Jeff Belmont. I saw him in the cellar. I went down the stairs, but I ended up here, in this place. The snow…" We'd reached the barn. The ground floor was big. There were ten horse stalls in the center of the open area. Four horses were tethered in the stalls. Bales of hay were piled along the outside walls. The barn had a strong odor of horse manure and cut grass. As I closed the door, I heard someone running down the hill towards us. The Continentals must have finished the job. I felt pleased. There would be no warning from the outpost this time. My mind flashed to Andy, but there was still work to be done here. I buttoned Mrs. Royce's coat as she was shaking her head trying to clear out the cobwebs.

"Do you remember Mr. Royce's work, the transporter that actually works like a time machine?"

"Yes, yes! Is that what happened to me?" She appeared to be warming up a little, and as she did, she become more alert. At least the barn kept the cold wind off her. We walked to the back where it seemed the warmest. I would have called Andy on the transmitter, but I didn't want to alarm his mom if he didn't or couldn't answer.

"Exactly. You were transported back in time to…" The door flew open but the man who stepped through wasn't any of my companions. One of the Hessians had escaped from the house! Where were the Continentals? Were they killed? At least I knew that the alarm couldn't have been given because he was the first to make it to the barn. He growled something in German when he saw me. We were several yards apart, and as I stood up, he appeared to back off. He could see that I was bigger, and he must have decided to escape rather than fight. He went for a horse.

This is what it came down to. I had to stop this last Hessian from sprinting off and alerting his army. I knew what to do, and this time, I didn't hesitate. I growled and charged at the man as he tried to mount the horse. I struck him like a tackle sacking a quarterback, and we both crashed through the railings that formed the horse stall. I landed on top of him in the dirt and when he didn't move, I released my grip figuring that I had knocked him out cold. I was wrong. The man was clever and was only playing possum. When I started to get up, he kicked me in the chest. The blow partially knocked the wind out of me, and I heard Mrs. Royce scream. The pain was excruciating, and I felt my legs wobble, but I managed to make it to my feet. The Hessian got to his feet, too and charged. I was ready for him and landed a blow square in his face before he reached me. His nose splattered blood all over the stall, but he was tough. I had stopped him only momentarily. He came at me again in an instant, and this time, he kept his head down protecting his newly broken nose. When he got close, I sidestepped and watched him glide by and stumble to the ground. I turned around, ready to pin the man when Mrs. Royce stepped in between us. She had her back to me and held a broken board from the stall railing that we crashed through a few seconds before. I hesitated as I saw the Hessian rise. Andy's mom didn't. In one motion, she brought the board, flat side down, on the top of the man's head as he tried to stand up. He immediately dropped to his knees. Then she wound up and clobbered him again. This time he pitched forward, face first, into the dirt–senseless. As I moved passed Mrs. Royce to stand over the fallen man, I heard someone clapping to my right. I looked over, and there in the doorway stood my four companions. They were bloody and dirty, but each sported an ear-to-ear grin.

"How long were ye there?" I asked, annoyed all of a sudden.

"Well, we'd perty near seed the whole thing," Sergeant Milbury replied.

"I take it he be that last of 'em. Ye didn't think ta lend a hand, eh?" I was getting into the dialect again, and as I said this, I gave Mrs. Royce a wink.

"We figg'r'd you'd like ta git one on your own. Anyway, it was a good way ta tell that you and this lady here ain't no spies. Iff'n ye wasn't here, he might of just made it. Now we can gag and hog-tie 'im, and leave him in this here barn. Ma'am, you'd best stay here, too. The army's on its way an' that there farm house ain't fit for a lady t'see iff'n ye know what I mean." With that he gave us a wink.

My four companions made sure that the Hessian was tied securely and could not cry out. In a fit of childish glee, they stuffed a road apple–a ball of hay filled with horse manure–into the man's mouth before applying the gag. My stomach did flip-flops at the thought, but I didn't say anything. Actually, I was sure that the man would consider himself fortunate to wake up with a bad taste in his mouth rather than dead. I could see that Mrs. Royce was having trouble with this as well, but she was smart enough not to interfere.

"I reckon we'd best be headin' back to the captain. He'll be needin' us soon," I said, then turning to Mrs. Royce, "we'll be back t'get ye afta the battle, ma'am. In the meantime, please stay out o' sight and make sure our friend stays quiet." She looked a little scared to be left alone in such strange surroundings, but I could tell that she understood, and after a moment, she nodded her head.

As we left the barn, I turned around one last time to give Andy's mom a wave. She returned it, and we made our way back up to the farmhouse and the Scotch Road. The men were excited after their encounter with the Hessians. They had a right to be. They had beaten professional soldiers in close quarters, hand-to-hand combat. They had the advantage of surprise, as the Continental army hoped to when they reached Trenton.

I was happy when I realized that the timeline was properly restored, but sad when I thought about Andy and Amy. What had happened to them? Amy was part of a world that no longer existed, and it was likely that she was gone. If Andy was removed from the protective area of the cellar was he gone, too? Did he turn off the time machine as he said he would? Are Mrs. Royce and I trapped in the past? I reached for the transmitter and realized that it was missing. I must have lost it when I took off my coat and put it around Mrs. Royce. I could no longer contact Andy even if I wanted to. Andy's mom and I were alone in 1776. I felt lost, but I couldn't dwell on my misfortune. The second division of the Continental army was in full view and marching toward us.

# Chapter 23—The Battle Of Trenton

"Glad to see that you men made it back. Was it a successful mission, Sergeant?" Captain Hamilton asked, after we'd backtracked through the advanced guard to reach his company of artillery.

"It appears so, sir. The woman was along the road just as young Mr. Walton said she'd be. He was right. She didn't have hardly a stitch on. She was cold, but she weren't no spy. She did wake up the Hessians in an outpost jist as we'd come up, but she wuz jist was tryin' to git out o' the snow, sir. She pitched in and hep'd us make sure them Hessian fellers didn't send the alarm, sir. Ain't that right, boys?" Various responses such as "that's so!" and "clobbered that fella good, she done!" were bantered around.

Hamilton was pleased and clapped me on the shoulder. "Glad to have you in our company, Mr. Walton. The general must think highly of you to send you on a mission as important as that." I smiled, realizing that the captain had no idea what my mission was.

We were still a few miles north of Trenton, but the army had momentum and was moving quickly. The sun was rising, and the snow that was falling earlier had turned to sleet again. I hoped that it wouldn't slow the army down. The noise of moving all the cannon, men, and ordinance sounded deafening to me as I marched with the column. It seemed inconceivable that the enemy could not hear us, but from my understanding from history class, it was likely that the Hessians were not in their finest form after yesterday's Christmas celebration. That fact, and the muffling effect of the snow, no doubt dulled their ability to detect us. That would not last for long.

The snow and the march had not dampened my companions' enthusiasm since the raid on the outpost. They must have told the story a dozen times to a hundred soldiers in the last hour. I was still thinking of the dead men and the fates of Amy, Andy, and Mrs. Royce, so I wasn't exactly in a celebratory mood. The sergeant and his men wrote it off as the usual reaction of a new kid seeing killing for the first time. It wasn't that of course. I'd seen plenty of slaughter at Gettysburg during my last trip into the past, and although I was still thoroughly sickened by it, I found that I could cope with it easier this time. Still, I didn't mind if the men thought I was new to it. I was marching once again into battle, and I knew that there'd be a lot more death before this day–heck, this morning–was through. But it was a battle that had to be fought. It was a battle that would save the Republic.

I lost track of time on the march, and it was full daylight when we heard the first clash of arms. The front of Greene's column had reached the Pennington Road and engaged the Hessian pickets. At once Captain Hamilton became excited and began urging the troops in front to move faster. Minutes later we saw the town before us.

The Hessians were rapidly falling back in the face of the superior number of Continental soldiers. Instead of retreating along the Pennington Road, the Hessians attempted to dash across the field to reach the town from just above the river. They were forced to change direction once again as more Continentals raced to meet them from the field to our right.

Farther away, near the Trenton waterfront, the soldiers under General Sullivan were driving a group of green-jacketed Hessians across a bridge that spanned a small creek. If they were supposed to alert their countrymen in the barracks, they were heading the wrong way. This small group was running itself out of the fight in a hurry!

In the column ahead of me, the first artillery units had pushed on and were now in position to fire along the town's main roads. The guns were placed on high ground, and from that vantage point, the officers' quarters, main barracks, and most of the buildings could be battered to pieces. Soon Captain Hamilton had some open space in his front as troops cleared the way by fanning out over the fields, and he immediately ordered his guns deployed next to the main batteries. As the enemy converged in the streets in an attempt to form ranks, Hamilton's shells could be seen exploding among them!

I stood transfixed as several Hessians raced to their cannon to return fire. They got off several shots but were soon stricken down by American riflemen. Continental troops raced over to capture the cannon minutes later.

The town was in chaos. More accurately, it was the Hessian soldier population that was behaving chaotically. The scene reminded me of science class when the chemistry teacher tried to explain the principles of the random motions of molecules in nature. It looked like that on a grand scale! Hessian soldiers in various stages of dress were running here and there in a hopeless attempt to organize. Clusters of Continentals could be seen moving through the maze, in orderly patterns, firing their rifles and making prodigious use of the bayonet. It was like watching a movie. The sites hardly seemed real!

The roar of cannon immediately in my front shook me back to reality, and I turned to see the troops of General Nathanael Greene's column pouring by us and into the town. With General Sullivan's men already occupying the riverfront, the Hessians had no choice but to surrender or flee into an apple orchard beyond the town. Many of them made it there, but it only delayed the inevitable as the orchard rapidly became surrounded by Greene's soldiers as well. A few may have slipped away, but it didn't change the fact that the rout was on!

I looked to my front and slightly left. A group of officers, in blue dress uniforms, was gathered outside a two story, wooden building that was serving as an officers' barracks. Smoke came from the structure, and it was impossible to tell in the haze whether artillery shells had struck the building, or if the smoke came from a fireplace inside. The officers appeared calm amid the battle that raged around them. The falling snow, and smoke from the fire, frequently obscured the group from my view. Out in front, one man appeared to be giving orders. I guessed that he was Colonel Johann Rall, the commander of the Hessian troops.

It was apparent that I wasn't the only one drawn to the group. The colonel had obviously become a target for some nearby riflemen. The man was shot as I watched! He staggered for a moment, bleeding from a chest wound, and fell to the ground. I didn't know if the man would survive, his wounds looked severe, but I was sure that the battle was over for him. His aide, and an attending officer, half dragged and half carried the stricken man to an adjacent building that had the appearance of a church. My only thought at that moment was that his men had brought him to the right place.

With the lost of Colonel Rall, the fight seemed to go out of the rest of the Hessians. Sometime later, I saw the first of several white flags that would make an appearance over the next half-hour. Mercifully, the enemy was surrendering. The battle was turning into a mopping up action for the Continentals. There would be no Hessian victory today!

I walked farther up the hill to improve my vantage point, and I caught a glimpse of General Washington. He was on horseback, and he was setting out to inspect the captured town. I maneuvered myself so that his path would take him near me. As he came, I waved my hands to get his attention.

"Ahoy there, General," I yelled. "Didn't I tell ye we would win?" To my shock and delight, the general steered his mount to my position.

"That you did, lad. I've got half a mind to put you on my staff! Where's your company? I'd like to congratulate you and the rest of your fellows. It was a great victory for all of us!" General Washington was speaking to me again!

"I've been with Captain Hamilton and the artillery, yonder," I replied, as I pointed to the cannon.

"Oh!" he said. "You're serving with a good man. Mr. Walton, wasn't it?" I nodded. "Well, your cannon is in a fine spot. It seems appropriate the artillery struck this great blow for democracy at the head of King and Queen Streets, doesn't it," he said as we both laughed. "Give Captain Hamilton my regards, and tell him that I shall be over to see him shortly," he said as he rode off.

I was elated! Imagine speaking to the great General George Washington twice in one day! Our mission to correct the timeline had been successful, but unlike the Continental army, we had suffered casualties. I thought of Amy and Whitman when I saw them last. They were willing to accept that their whole world would be lost if we were successful, and they freely gave their very existence to help us. Andy faced the same fate if he had been trapped outside his basement when the timeline changed. Mrs. Royce and I were looking at exile in 1776.

Yet the future was saved. Nazi's would not be conquering Europe. The Japanese would be expelled from the Asian mainland, and the world would once again enter the twenty-first century with democracy as the foremost government. The future was saved, and the price had to be worth it.

As I returned to relay my message from General Washington to Captain Hamilton, I saw the dark side of war. The wounded and the bodies of the dead were being rifled for loot. In addition, some men had found liquor among the Hessians' supplies and were helping themselves to generous quantities. Considering what they'd been through over the last few months, and especially the last few hours, I supposed that this development was inevitable. Maybe they were entitled to blow off a little steam. Captain Hamilton was speaking with some artillery officers as I arrived. He and his companions gave low and exaggerated bows as I approached.

"You seem to be on the most friendly terms with our commander, Mr. Walton," the captain said with a wide grin.

"Yes. It would seem, sir, that he values my military opinion greatly," I replied attempting to out do him in the grin department. "Also, the general says that he will be over to see you soon, Captain. As you may expect, he is quite delighted with the outcome of the battle."

Earlier, just before the final surrender of the Hessians, I watched as Colonel Rall was carried from the church to a building across the road. Now, Captain Hamilton and I looked up and saw the general dismount and enter that building. I suspected that General Washington intended to pay his respects to his fallen adversary. It was hard to believe, but the whole battle lasted slightly more than an hour and a half. It was, however, long enough to change the course of history.

With the officers occupied assessing the damage and handling prisoners, and the men relaxing, looting, or getting drunk, I saw my opportunity to slip back to the farmhouse and find Mrs. Royce. The walk would give me time to think of a plan to begin our new lives in Colonial America. I slipped off easily enough. I passed several stragglers still making their way to town, and on each occasion I was compelled to retell the story of the Battle of Trenton. More than once I saw a hint of regret in a soldier's eye for being late and missing the show. I felt like a war veteran, and I found myself thinking that maybe the experience would teach these laggards something, and the next time they would try harder to keep up. I realized that this was harsh criticism, and not every man can stand the physical demands of a campaign such as this–especially men worn out from months of fighting and marching under starvation conditions. Some straggling is inevitable and not a sign of cowardice.

The sky was brighter when I reached the farmhouse. The sky was still cloudy, but the sleet was tapering off. I was gripped by a sudden fear that something was wrong! I had no evidence, but the fear was real. I quickly ran around to the back and entered the barn through the only door. It took a second to adjust to the dim light. I expected to be reassured that everything was the same as when we left, but it wasn't. Mrs. Royce was gone! I yelled her name several times. Nothing! I ran outside and yelled some more. Still nothing! I even went into the farmhouse. The bodies of the Hessian soldiers were pale. Their dead eyes were glazed over and congealed blood was everywhere. I was sure that Mrs. Royce would not be in there. Was she hurt? Did she run off? No chance of that I realized. Had someone taken her away? That could happen, and the thought of it filled me with dread. I realized that our captured friend might have some answers, so I decided to return to the barn.

The prisoner was exactly as we left him. Not exactly, I realized. The road apple had been removed from his mouth. I suspected that Andy's mom did that as soon as we left. She reapplied the gag, though. He was awake and alert, and I was happy to see that he appeared to be unharmed. Since the battle was over, I saw no reason to leave him bound. I untied his gag and was about to ask him about Mrs. Royce, when he began to jabber hysterically. He wasn't shouting, but it was clear the man had seen something that severely rattled him. Unfortunately, I couldn't understand any of it. He was speaking entirely in German. I figured that he was trying to tell me something about Mrs. Royce because I heard *frau*–the German word for woman–several times, but without a translator I was getting nowhere. I felt fortunate that the man knew something, and I realized that my best hope was to take him back to Trenton and find someone who could tell me what he was saying. I began to untie the man's feet when I suddenly felt a strange, tingling sensation. I stood up and sensed the beginnings of the green haze as it enveloped me. The last thing I saw was the Hessian's face. His eyes were open wide in wonder, and he stared open-mouthed as I faded away. I realized in an instant that the man was witnessing this phenomenon for the *second* time! I hoped that he would recover from the shock. I also didn't know what I would find when I returned!

# Chapter 24—A Surprise At Home

I came to in a heap on the platform in Andy's cellar. I was very groggy and annoyed with myself for not having the presence of mind to lie down when I first saw the green haze. That would at least have saved me the pain of the fall. Of course, it would help if I knew when I was going to be transported! As my head cleared, I became conscious of the presence of several people. I recognized the first voice right away.

"Well, I'm glad to see that you made it okay, buddy. We lost contact for awhile, and we were afraid that we'd be bringing back a bloody corpse." It was Andy! He was free! I was thrilled. I turned over to see if Mrs. Royce was okay, and I saw her smiling face looking back at me. No bruises either.

"Oh, Mark, I was so worried!" she said as she stroked my face. "I heard the fighting, and it took everything I had not to go after you. Are you really okay? Andy told me everything." I nodded, but with the release of the tension and the knowledge that Andy and his mom were back and well, I couldn't help but cry tears of joy! I sobbed as I thought of Amy, and it took a minute or so to gather the strength to rise.

"Is everything okay? Has history been corrected?" I asked.

"As far as we can tell, history is exactly as it was before," Andy replied.

"Did you see the baseball field?" I asked, knowing that would be one of the first things that Andy would look for, and it would confirm that the past had been restored.

He shot a puzzled look at his mom and asked, "The what?" Oh, no! Something went wrong! Andy and his mom could see the shocked look on my face, and it was Mrs. Royce who broke down.

"Okay, Andy, that's enough. We didn't have time to go to the baseball field, Mark, but I'm sure that it's right where you boys left it. Andy has a sick sense of humor sometimes," she said as she playfully slapped him on the back of the head.

"Actually, I was hoping that *you* would show me this baseball field." I recognized the voice, but it *couldn't* be! Andy and his mom stepped aside to give me a full view of Amy standing in front of the computer! I was stunned and overcome with joy. I vaulted off the platform and gave her a hug. She smiled as she kissed me.

I turned to Andy and asked, "Andy, how? *How* did you do this?" Then looking at Amy I said, "I thought that you went into the woods to stop the military police. Andy, I thought that *you* were captured, too."

"Oh give us a little credit for some brains," Andy said. "The last thing that I heard from you was that you spotted someone banging on a farmhouse door. We both figured that it was Mom, remember." I nodded my head. "Well, I ran outside and brought Amy and Mom back into the cellar, where as you can see, we made good use of some of the spare furniture and equipment in here." He pointed at the door to the backyard. It was barricaded with everything that wasn't bolted down. "I knew that it wouldn't take much to push the stuff out of the way, but I figured that it would take them a few minutes to decide what to do next. They assumed that we had no way out, and as a result, they didn't have any sense of time urgency. A few minutes later, they were gone. It was eerie. One second we could hear yelling from the outside, the next nothing but quiet. Also, the rest of the house is back!" Andy said as he pointed upstairs to the door. "Care for a soda?"

"Sure, I'd love one," I said as Andy started up the stairs.

"I'll get a round for all of us," he answered as he opened the door.

"Mrs. Royce, are you okay?" I asked. She looked the same as when I left her in the barn. I was thankful for that, because the last time I saw her in this cellar, she was badly bruised from the beating she received at the hands of the Hessians.

"I'm fine, Mark, thanks to you. I'm afraid that I scared that poor Hessian prisoner badly when I started to disappear. Did you see him again?"

"Actually I did," I said as I started to laugh. "You're right, you did scare him to death. He was still babbling about it when I returned to the barn. At least he was until he saw *me* disappear a few minutes later!" Mrs. Royce started laughing all over again when she heard that. Amy was looking at both of us like we'd grown extra heads.

"What do you remember about the past, Mrs. Royce? I mean from the time you reached the farmhouse?" I had a reason for asking; there was still something confusing about all this and it was making me uneasy.

"Only that I was freezing, and you found me on the porch and gave me that coat," she said as she pointed at the coat plopped in a heap on the cellar floor. Then she lowered her eyes. "I remember the Hessians and the blood and the fight in the barn. After the prisoner was tied up, I waited. I heard the cannon roar, and I was terrified that you'd be hurt. A few minutes later and I was here." Andy had returned with the sodas.

I looked at him and started to ask, "Did you tell..."

"He did, Mark, and I'm sorry for putting you at risk like that. I had no idea that Jeff Belmont had started the transporter before I stepped onto the platform."

"Oh, that's okay, Mrs. Royce. There was no way that you could have known that. At least we fixed it and had a great adventure at the same time!" Andy didn't tell her the whole story. He didn't tell her about the beating.

"I guess you're right, Mark. I'm going upstairs to make some sandwiches. I'll bet everyone is hungry about now." All three of us yelled a loud "Yes" at the same time. When she was upstairs and out of earshot, I turned to Andy again.

"You didn't tell her about the beating."

"No, because it never happened to her. Don't you see? She has no memory of any of that. In fact, Mom changed just as the timeline was restored. Her bruises were gone.

Amy came over to me. "He's right, Mark. There's no reason to tell her about that."

Andy continued, "As I was explaining what happened, I had to tell her about the change in the timeline. She felt terrible to have caused all this trouble, but I think I convinced her that it wasn't her fault, and that she shouldn't blame herself. Besides, the timeline was restored." All that was true, and I certainly didn't want to cause Mrs. Royce any pain by telling her about something that I was fortunate enough to prevent, but I was still puzzled by something that I couldn't put my finger on.

"I don't want to hurt your mom, Andy, you know that. It's just that there are some things that I don't understand," I said, shaking my head.

"Let me see if I can help," Andy offered.

"We determined that the cellar area was immune to changes in the timeline because it was so close to the interdimensional wormhole, right?" I asked.

"Okay so far," he answered.

"Well, Amy's here because she was in this protected area when the timeline changed."

"Right again."

"Your mom was in the same place, yet her memory has changed. That's the part that is bothering me. If everything in the cellar was protected from changes in the timeline, then why doesn't your mom remember her previous experience with the Hessians?"

"Oh, is that's all you want? That's *easy*," Andy said. I must have looked at him funny because he quickly added, "I didn't mean it like that. This *can* be confusing."

"Mom was in the protected area all right," he began as he held out his hands to illustrate the cellar, "but she didn't *need* to be. Keep in mind that she *belongs* in this timeline." I must have still looked confused. "Think of it like this, your mom and dad and Katie weren't in the cellar, but when you go home, you'll find them just as if nothing had happened, right?"

I wasn't getting it, but I had another thought. "*Andy, I've got to call home*! My folks must think I'm dead or something!" I yelled and started to move toward the stairs. Andy grabbed me from behind by the belt loop.

"Easy, big guy, you don't have to call home, I'm getting to that." I turned around.

"I've been gone for nearly two *days*! You don't think they've missed me by now!" I was a little shocked, and maybe a little hurt, but Andy went on.

"It hasn't been two days for them," he said. My jaw dropped as Andy continued, "Here, let's get the bench and sit down." The three of us pulled the bench off the heap that was barricading the door to the outside. We placed it in its usual spot in front of the computer. I sat in the middle with Amy on my left and Andy on my right.

"Okay, let's try this again," I said. In fact, I was relieved to find out that I wasn't going to be missed. I was afraid that my folks would kill me for disappearing for so long. I knew enough about Andy to trust his facts. I only hoped that he could explain this reasoning to me in my seemingly thick-headed condition. It was apparent that Andy found this whole outcome totally logical.

"All right, a person experiences time in one direction, from the past to the present to the future."

"Except for me on these trips," I said, figuring that I'd be smart.

"*No!*" Andy shouted. "Even *you* on these trips. You may be have been picked up and put somewhere else along the timeline, but *time*, as you see it, is still moving forward." I must be dumb because I still couldn't understand. I shook my head.

"Think of a leaf floating down a river. It goes ten feet, and then you pick it up, bring it back, and let it go ten feet again. How far has the leaf really gone?" he asked. Oh, oh, a trick question. I bit.

"Well, the leaf floated ten feet the first trip and ten feet the second trip, so I'd say twenty feet." I knew *that* had to be right.

"*Exactly*!" Andy exclaimed. "But *relative* to the shore, it only went ten feet." That made sense. I was beginning to see what he was getting at.

"Okay, I think I understand now. I was physically moved back in time, but for me, I was still moving forward. Like the leaf."

"Right. You remember the events in a straight line also. Two days ago, you were playing baseball with me in the twenty-first century, yesterday you were looking for Mom in 1776, and today you're back home near the time that you started. To you, those events happened one after the other."

"So yesterday, your mom saw Jeff Belmont down here in the cellar, three hours ago she was trying to keep from freezing in 1776, and now she's back in the twenty-first century making us sandwiches. I think I get it now. She doesn't remember the beating because her personal timeline was changed, and to her, it never happened."

"That's it. And we remember because it happened as one event after another to us." It was Amy; she was getting into it as well.

Andy continued, "That brings me to the next part. Take the leaf and put it into the river, then let it float ten feet. Pick up the leaf and bring it back. Now how far did the leaf move?"

It was Amy who answered this time. "The leaf moved ten feet, but from shore it looked like it didn't move at all because it was returned to its original position."

"That's right!" Andy said. "And that's what happened to us. We were the leaves, and time is the river. The starting point on the shore was the date and time that we ran into the cellar and saw someone go into the past."

"Okay, I'm with you so far." I was scaring myself because as really *was* beginning to get it. "You're saying that we lived two days, but the actual date hasn't moved at all. Is that it?"

"It appears that way," Andy said. "I checked my upstairs computer as soon as the timeline changed back. According to its clock only a few minutes had passed, and that was about as long as it took to go upstairs and boot it up. I'm willing to bet that no time had passed. So you see, Mark, your family wouldn't have missed you yet."

I still wasn't clear about something. "The last trip–to Gettysburg–I spent twenty-four hours in the past, but when I returned, twenty-four hours had passed here, too. How do you explain that?"

Andy shrugged, "That time nothing of significance had changed. You were living on a timeline that was parallel to this one. When you came back, you simply moved into your previous timeline where you would have been if you didn't leave. This time, our world was destroyed. When it was restored, it had to restart from where it left off." Andy gave a sort of grin that I'd seen before. He was formulating this theory as he went along.

"You're making that up! You don't know for sure why our timeline didn't move this time, do you?" I knew I was right because Andy got defensive.

"Well, facts are facts. It's exactly the same time as when we stepped into the cellar–plus the time it took to talk about all this, of course. Do you have a better explanation?"

I didn't, and I knew that was as close as I was going to get to an admission from Andy that he wasn't sure how it all worked out.

"Well, *I'm* not going to quibble over a couple of days," Amy said. "When are you gentlemen going to show the new kid around?" At that moment, Andy's mom yelled downstairs that the sandwiches were ready.

"How about right after lunch?"

# Epilogue

Andy and I had a terrific time showing Amy the sights of her new hometown. She marveled at the increased population, and the speed of the traffic on the Southeast Expressway. (I chose to show her the highway before the bumper-to-bumper traffic of rush hour!) But most of all, she was impressed by the lack of an evening curfew and the general air of peace and prosperity. On a walk through French's Common we came across a young couple carrying a toddler and pushing an infant in a baby carriage. Amy cried tears of joy knowing that the kids' dad wouldn't be required to die fighting in an African desert.

I was happy that Amy would be staying with us. The Royces were kind enough to take her into their home, and Andy and I began her training in world history post 1776. She loved the challenge and made many interesting observations that we had never stopped to consider. I remember one evening, as we prepared to cruise my version of the South Shore Plaza, when she stated out of the blue that the United States Constitution was a remarkable document. When I asked why she thought that, she stated that the authors–I often had to remind her that we usually referred to them as the founding fathers–had identified a way to deal with every situation that could possibly come up. For those issues that couldn't be anticipated in the Republic's infancy, they devised the amendment process. It created a sort of organic government that evolves to maintain its relevance as it holds certain core elements inviolate. The executive, judiciary, and legislative branches of the government must always remain in place, but through the workings of those branches, amendments can be added altering the laws themselves. I knew about that, but I never had it explained to me in such an interesting and concise manner.

Amy has her favorite historical figures as well. Thomas Jefferson, our third president, had the insight to make the Louisiana Purchase after a shortsighted congress arrogantly proclaimed that the United States had plenty of expansion room and didn't need any land west of the Mississippi. Sam Houston, the principle founder of the Republic of Texas, unselfishly gave up the Texas presidency and successfully pressed the United States congress to annex his country and make it a U. S. state. Teddy Roosevelt, William H. Taft, and Woodrow Wilson showed that the constitutional government would not stand idly by as industrial robber barons and their monopolies pillaged the American people for personal gain.

But the figure she admired most was Winston Churchill, England's iron prime minister during World War II, who single-handedly galvanized an empire that, with U.S. help, stopped the Nazis from over running Europe in the twentieth-century's darkest hour. His strong personal bond with President Franklin D. Roosevelt ensured that the two countries would fight for the common cause of democracy until the world was free of tyranny. Also, because his mother was an American and his father British, he represented to Amy a unification of her adopted country with the country of her birth.

Amy didn't miss the tragic periods of our history. She was disappointed that the United States tolerated slavery long after the rest of the civilized world outlawed it, and she was saddened that the "peculiar institution" led to a brutal and wasteful civil war. She learned about the Watergate scandal that virtually shutdown the government in the middle 1970s and next to the Civil War, may have been the greatest constitutional crisis our Republic has faced.

Sometimes when we are together in the library, I'll see Amy smile as she reads some historical passage, or the recollection of some event, and I'll wonder what caught her fancy. When asked, she'll relate a story of a family who gave up everything to build a new life as pioneers in the American west, or of an invention that someone first made in a garage and is now a household name. She confessed to me once that she understood how the people who left their homes to come to the United States must have felt as they viewed the American shore for the first time. Although she was born on this land, she was indeed looking at America for the first time, and like the immigrants before her, she was filled with the same hope that she, too, could build a new and exciting future.

As Americans, we often take opportunity for granted. We live everyday with the confidence that comes from seeing our nation, and its people, overcome adversity and achieve greatness. Our success stories are common, and our heroes can be found in every walk of life. It therefore gave me a renewed feeling of pride to think that the promise of this country had touched another life, and one to which I felt so close. She marveled that the freedom that the constitution guarantees has allowed our nation to build the greatest industrial, economic, and military power the world has ever seen. This government has proven to work through times of war, peace, economic depression, and everything in between. With the proper vision and leadership, we seem to be able to achieve almost anything. And yes, Amy, Americans have even walked on the moon!

## *The Preamble of the United States Constitution*

*We the People of the United States, in Order to form a more perfect Union, establish Justice, insure domestic Tranquility, provide for the common defence, promote the general Welfare, and secure the Blessings of Liberty to ourselves and our Posterity, do ordain and establish this Constitution for the United States of America.*

# AUTHOR'S NOTE

To the Reader,

I have always believed that throughout recorded history there have been but a handful of single events that have altered the pathway of human political evolution. I would put the Battle of Trenton in this category. It is not an exaggeration to say that before dawn on December 26, 1776, the world's first modern independent republic teetered on the brink of extinction. A loss at Trenton and a subsequent collapse of the Revolution would have put an end to the noble experiment virtually before it started. With democracy suffering such a setback, generations may have passed before an embolden populous would again rise up to overthrow a monarchy. Fortunately for us, Washington's skillful leadership–and the enemy's inattention–insured that we'd never know.

Factual information for this story came from several sources, but it was from the book *The Battles of Trenton and Princeton* by William S. Stryker that I took the main points. This work, considered by many to be the definitive written history of the battle, provides extraordinary detail concerning the disposition of the combatants, weather conditions, timing of troop movements, terrain, and myriad other particulars that shaped events. In addition to American reports, Stryker researched actual Hessian records to corroborate or debunk traditional thinking. This added a dimension that was heretofore missing, and it contributed to a more comprehensive and accurate version of the battle.

Of my other sources, *The Patriots*, written by A. J. Langguth, gave an excellent overview of the battle and its importance to the Revolution in general, and the motion picture, *The Crossing*, produced by the Arts and Entertainment network, demonstrated visually the logistics and technical challenges that Washington and Knox faced in bringing the Continental army across the Delaware River in a winter storm. Still, I felt that I needed to see the site in person to answer some detailed questions, and for that I traveled to Washington Crossing State Park. It was here that I met W. Clay Craighead, Historic Preservation Specialist. Mr. Craighead was a great help in providing data to plug some holes in my research, and it was he who informed me that Stryker's book had been reprinted and was available at the Old Barracks Museum–a fact that proved to be informational gold!

A question that has been asked for over two centuries is: How could such disciplined troops as the Hessians, under such a capable commander as Colonel Johann Rall, be caught so totally by surprise? This seems especially incredible considering the attack was delayed until daylight!

One reason was that the winter storm made it easier for the Hessians to relax their guard, and in fact, they failed to send out adequate patrols. Patrols would almost certainly have discovered the movements of the Continental Army and returned to sound the alarm. The weather also served to dull any sounds made by the soldiers' approach.

A second reason could be Washington's choice of the day of the attack. Christmas Day was a traditional day of celebration for Germans, so the general could have reasonably assumed that their degree of readiness and response time following such a festival may have been substandard.

Or a third reason, which I believe is the primary factor that ensured that the Hessians would be caught off guard: the total contempt in which Colonel Rall held the Continental Army. He believed that Washington's men were of no account, and although he knew that the Continentals held superior numbers, he refused to even entertain the possibility of an attack. A more thoughtful commander may have considered that an adversary who was freezing and starving in the Pennsylvania woods might be driven to try an act of desperation. Given that idea, the Christmas holiday may be a prime occasion. But Rall gave no thought to such things.

The facts indicate that the colonel was urged by a trusted officer to check all ferry crossings following a skirmish on Christmas night, yet Rall steadfastly refused. Later, as Rall was drinking wine and playing cards, the movements of the Continental Army *were* discovered. The warning, in the form of a note from a local Tory, was passed directly to him in plenty of time to confirm the intelligence and prepare, but instead, he put the note in his pocket without reading it. He did read it later, but only after the battle was lost and he was mortally wounded.

Whether it was the storm, the Christmas festivities, or Rall's arrogance, the Continental Army did surprise the Hessians and win a great victory on December 26, 1776. And in doing so, the army got the supplies that it desperately needed. It was the battle that renewed the country's hope. It was the battle that saved the American Revolution.

Mark refers to the famous painting *Washington Crossing the Delaware* as an historically inaccurate depiction of the actual event. While this is true, it's possible that the artist, Emanuel Gottlieb Leutze, had something else in mind. If he wanted to create an image of Washington as a great leader–standing tall in the face of adversity as he brought his country, and the world, into the dawning era of democracy–Leutze certainly succeeded. At least that's what I think of when I view the painting, and that's why I wanted it on the cover.

Amy was introduced to provide a reasonable and easy interface between Andy & Mark's world and British North America. I was also happy that Andy had the insight to bring her along when the timeline was restored to normal. Look for Amy's quick intelligence, natural curiosity, and sense of adventure as she joins the boys in the next story–*Custer's Last Stand!*

To Parents and Teachers,

The site where the Continental Army crossed the Delaware River on the night of December 25, 1776 can still be seen today. McKonkey's Ferry, where the army disembarked, is preserved as part of the Washington Crossing Historic Park in Pennsylvania. The point where the army landed, Johnson's Ferry in New Jersey, is at Washington Crossing State Park. A small bridge makes it easy to travel from one side to the other. The grounds of both riversides are in beautiful park-like settings, and both parks cater to families and school field trips.

My wife and I spent several hours walking the grounds. We had a great day, and the children we met thoroughly enjoyed themselves. Since we chose a sunny, warm, spring day, we could only imagine what it must have been like for Washington and his men to suffer through the icy crossing then form up and march the eight miles to Trenton. Maybe we'll go back in the winter and try it. Well, maybe not!

The history of British North America, as Andy explains it to Mark, is, of course, pure speculation, but I must admit that I had a lot of fun writing it. The "what if" analysis is one of my favorite techniques for encouraging kids to open up during a discussion. I think it works because everyone can take comfort in the fact that there can be no wrong answers. It's great for exercising the imagination, and the responses range from the insightful to the hysterical! If you haven't tried this one, I highly recommend it!

-W. F. Reed

# About the Author

W. F. Reed is a chemical cngineer in the semiconductor industry and mathematics and chemistry tutor at Framingham State College in Massachusetts.

0-595-23587-5